Also by Jan Henson Dow

Nonfiction
Writing the Award-Winning Play (with Shannon Michal
  Dow.)

Poetry
At the Han-ku Pass

Short Plays
*Plays that Pop!: One-Act, Ten-Minute, and Mono-
  logues*

Full-Length Plays
Dark Passages (with Shannon Michal Dow and Robert
  Schroeder, published by Popular Play Service.)
Dreamers, Shadows, Dreams (with Robert Schroeder,
  published by Phosphene Publishing Co.)
The Golden Dawn (with Robert Schroeder, published by
  Phosphene Publishing Co.)
Killing Dante (with Shannon Michal Dow, published by
  Samuel French, Inc.)
The Magistry (with Robert Schroeder, published by Popular
  Play Service.)
The Moorlark (with Shannon Michal Dow, published by
  Phosphene Publishing Co.)
Shaka (with Robert Schroeder, published by Phosphene
  Publishing Co.)
That Madcap Moon (with Robert Schroeder, published by
  Phosphene Publishing Co.)

The Golden Dawn

The Golden Dawn

A Play by

Jan Henson Dow
&
Robert Schroeder

Phosphene Publishing Company
Houston, Texas

The Golden Dawn
© 2017 by Jan Henson Dow
ISBN 10: 0-9986316-1-2
ISBN 13: 978-0-9986316-1-5

Published by
Phosphene Publishing Company
Houston, Texas, USA
phosphenepublishing.com

1.1

Cover: The Rosy Cross worn by Adepts in the Rosae Rubae et Aureae Crucis, the inner order of the Hermetic Order of the Golden Dawn.

For all my grandchildren:

Heather, Carly, Will, and Ben Hauser
Sydney Dow Göehl and Mariko Dow Osegueda
Brendan and Ian Ward

Production of *The Golden Dawn*

This edition of *The Golden Dawn* is dedicated to the reading public only. Professionals and amateurs are hereby warned that the play is subject to production fees. All rights, including professional, amateur, motion pictures, recitation, lecturing, public reading, radio broadcasting, television, and the rights of translation into foreign languages, are strictly reserved.

The amateur live stage performance rights to *The Golden Dawn* are controlled exclusively by Phosphene Publishing Company. There is a fee of $35 to produce this play, and the fee must be paid and rights secured in writing from Phosphene Publishing Company at least two weeks prior to the opening performance of the play. The fee must be paid whether the play is presented for charity or by a nonprofit or profit-seeking organization and whether or not admission is charged.

Professional and stock royalty will be quoted on application to Phosphene Publishing Company.

Copying from this book without express permission of the publisher is strictly forbidden by law, and the right of performance is not transferable.

Whenever the play is produced, the following notice must appear on all programs, printing, and advertising for the play: "Produced by special arrangement with Phosphene Publishing Company."

Due authorship credit must be given on all programs, printing, and advertising for the play.

No one shall commit or authorize any act or omission by which the copyright, or the right to copyright, of this play may be impaired.

No one may make any changes to this play in the process of production, or otherwise.

Correspondence and inquiries may be made through the Phosphene Publishing Company website at phosphenepublishing.com.

The Golden Dawn

Cast of Characters
(In order of appearance)

ALEISTER CROWLEY, mid-twenties, but appears older. He is of medium height and good physique, evidence of his passion for hiking and mountain-climbing. His piercing, intense eyes evidence his magnetic personality. He will later become notorious as a Magus of black magic. (Crowley is pronounced "crow-lee.")

FLORENCE FARR EMERY, early thirties, the determinedly liberated Victorian actress. Dynamic and very good looking, but dresses without care or calculation. George Bernard Shaw said of Florence: "She was in violent reaction against Victorian morals, especially sexual and domestic morals."

WILLIAM BUTLER YEATS, early thirties, but seems younger. He is slim, dark, intense, and has not yet become a famous poet. He has a shock of dark hair that falls over his forehead.

WILLIAM SHARP / FIONA MacLEOD (played by the same actor), late thirties. Sharp, male, a noted critic, is slim, of medium height, and handsome, but his manner is stiff and stilted, and he is pedantic and smug. He carries a cane in an affected manner. Fiona, seemingly female, who has become a famous author of the Celtic twilight, gives the impression of mystery and grace, but hidden beauty. Fiona and Sharp are two halves of a split personality, but this has not been revealed at the time depicted in this play. [Regarding the performance program: Different names should be listed as the actors playing William Sharp and Fiona MacLeod in order to avoid telegraphing the play's denouement to the audience.]

BRAM STOKER, early fifties, looks like one's favorite uncle and is very respectably the British gentleman. He is manager of Lyceum Theatre and the author of *Dracula*.

MAUD GONNE, early thirties, famous spokesperson for Irish revolution and reputed to be one of the most beautiful women of her time. She is tall, proud, regal, and charismatic and dresses at all times in the height of fashion. Her accent is cosmopolitan and without a brogue despite her Irish revolutionary stance.

Time and Place
The year 1900, London, England

The Set
The single set represents variously:

The basic set represents the meeting room of the Isis-Urania Temple of The Order of the Golden Dawn, in London. The Victorian room is dark-paneled and sparsely furnished with a sofa, several chairs, and a wall cabinet. The cabinet's contents include a wine decanter, wine glasses, and candelabra. DL, a fireplace is ready to be lit.

Upstage center are hinged panels. When they are opened, they form screens paralleling the two side walls of the main room, hiding the dark paneling and revealing the brightly decorated Inner Vault. The Inner Vault evinces a dramatically different mood from that of the main room. The ceiling of the Vault is tilted upward, so the audience can see the pure-white ceiling. In its center is a large rose almost covering a gold cross, both enclosed within a black triangle—the whole surrounded by a black heptagram.

Each panel of the Vault's back wall is painted a different color, in a spectrum based on that of a rainbow. Zodiacal, planetary, chemical, and cabalistic symbols, along with Hebrew letters, are displayed on the back panels. The panels on either side of the opening to the Vault are painted with the Tree of Life entwined by a red, seven-headed dragon.

At each side, in the rear of the Inner Vault, are two tall columns—one white, one black. At the center of the Vault is a six-sided altar. When the altar is rolled back, a six-sided coffin is revealed. This is the coffin Fiona is discovered lying in in Act II: Scene Four. The base of the coffin rises when activated, creating the effect of Fiona being levitated.

Hanging just behind and above the altar is a golden bell which gives off a sweet, haunting sound. Atop the altar, centered, is a large golden chalice. A sword lies before it. A crook and a wand are at either side. Candles are on each side of the chalice.

Other vignetted locales, as outlined in the Synopsis of Scenes, below.

Costumes
Fashionable attire, circa 1900 in London, England.

Act I: Scene One
Crowley, Sharp, and Stoker are in "correct" evening attire. Florence is simply and casually dressed in an afternoon dress of no special distinction. She has not changed for the evening. Yeats is rather obviously dressed as the "poet," in a somewhat theatrical cloak worn over a short jacket and in a flowing bow tie. Maud, who flaunts the gowns of the couturiers of her time, is dressed for the evening in the height of fashion. Although Fiona appears in a long black dress and cloak, with a black hat, black veil, and black gloves, the effect is that of subdued beauty and grace. When Crowley, Florence, Yeats, Stoker, and Maud dress for the ritual, they all wear floor-length black robes and black half-masks. When Fiona dresses for the ritual, she wears a floor-length gray robe, and a gray veil covers her head and falls to her waist.

Act II: Scene One
Florence is casually dressed for the afternoon, while Maud is sharply fashionable.

Act II: Scene Two
Both Fiona and Crowley are dressed as in Act I: Scene One.

Act II: Scene Three
While Florence and Maud are both dressed for the afternoon, their manner of dress is again in sharp contrast. Yeats is still the "poet." Crowley and Stoker are dressed less formally than before. Sharp is dressed as in Act I: Scene One.

Act II: Scene Four
Before donning their same ritual attire, Yeats and Maud are dressed for traveling. The others are in the ritual attire worn in Act I: Scene One.

Synopsis of Scenes

Act I
Scene One: The meeting room. 8:00 PM.

Act II
Scene One: Florence's sitting room. The following afternoon.
Scene Two: The meeting room. A few hours later.
Scene Three: The meeting room. The following afternoon.
Scene Four: The meeting room, with the panels to the Inner Vault now open. A day later, just before midnight.

The Golden Dawn

ACT I: SCENE ONE

(The meeting room of the Isis-Urania Temple of the Order of the Golden Dawn, London. The hinged panels UC are closed. The time is 8:00 pm. The year is 1900. ALEISTER CROWLEY enters DR. HE is in evening dress. CROWLEY quickly looks around the room. HE goes to the door at DL, looks into the adjoining room. He starts to cross R. He hears noises off, turns, and exits DL, leaving the door open slightly so he can hear the conversation. CROWLEY's reactions to what follows are visible to the audience. WILLIAM BUTLER YEATS and FLORENCE FARR EMERY enter DR. YEATS, rather obviously dressed as "the poet," wears a shabby jacket with a flowing bow tie. Over his clothes, he wears a long black robe. FLORENCE is dressed without care or calculation and also wears a long black robe. BOTH carry censers wafting incense as they circle the room. After circling the room, THEY stop UC.)

YEATS
(Intoning.)
All is ready for the initiation ceremony of The Order of the Golden Dawn.

(YEATS takes the censer from FLORENCE then

crosses to place both censers on the cabinet. THEY
remove their robes in silence. YEATS places HIS over
a chair. FLORENCE crosses to the DL door. Without entering the off-stage room, SHE further opens
its door, and places her robe just within the open door.
SHE does not see CROWLEY, though the audience
does. YEATS, now speaks in a casual tone. While HE
takes pride in, and emotional sustenance from, HIS
Irish heritage, there is nothing of the brogue in HIS
manner of speaking. He speaks as would an educated
British gentleman of HIS time.)
How many of us will be there tonight?

FLORENCE
Only a few of us, I'm afraid. Dr. Westcott sends his regrets—called
away on business.

YEATS
Called away on business! Is he a member of this Order or not?

FLORENCE
And Emily has to attend her mother's gout.

YEATS
I wish Emily's mother would attend her own gout for a change. Any
more letters from out "Supreme Wizard" Mathers?

FLORENCE
(Hesitantly.)
Four came this week.

YEATS
Why didn't you tell me?

FLORENCE
You just got back. I didn't want to upset you.

YEATS

Well, you have upset me. Are you the secretary of this Order or not?

FLORENCE

Now, Willie. I am, but....

YEATS

Then, as leader of this Order, I would appreciate receiving my letters, so I can at least know what Mathers is plotting now.

FLORENCE

Don't let him upset you so. I think Mathers has been too long in Paris. He's losing his grip on reality.

YEATS

God, I'm tired of this endless squabbling!

FLORENCE

You've been working too hard, Willie. You try to take everything on your own shoulders.

YEATS

I can't be in two places at once—Dublin and London! In Dublin, I'm trying to found an Irish National Theatre with no money and little support and endless squabbling! And here in London, I'm trying to keep The Order of the Golden Dawn from being torn apart by more endless squabbling! I thought I could at least depend on you to handle things here!

FLORENCE

You can depend on me, Willie. You know that.

YEATS

(Angrily.)

Can I?

FLORENCE
(Appealingly.)
Willie!

YEATS
Oh, Florence, forgive me. I'm—on edge. I shouldn't take it out on you. I spend all my time trying to make order of this chaos, while my own creative work goes begging!

FLORENCE
You're just tired. If I know you, you'll soon be your old self again, all full of dreams and visions for changing the world.

YEATS
Yes. Dreams and visions. That's all they are.

FLORENCE
You are a great poet, Willie. That counts for everything!

YEATS
Great poet! What a joke! Oh, yes, I write very pretty poems, but who finally gives a damn? I can see my obituary now: "William Butler Yeats, minor poet of the Celtic twilight and the mystic vision."

FLORENCE
You're being too hard on yourself, as usual.

YEATS
Am I? Sometimes I just want to go away—to get away. Live in some cabin somewhere like Thoreau. Once I saw a rabbit, old and lame, limping down a path into the woods. It was autumn. Death was in the air. I feel that autumn in my bones, now, nothing I dreamed of accomplished.

FLORENCE
I've never seen you so depressed.

YEATS

Don't you see, Florence? I feel the world is about to plunge into dark night, darker than it has ever known before, and only our light can hold back the darkness. That's why I can't give up. I don't dare give up.

FLORENCE

I would be more than your "eternal optimist." You know that, Willie.

YEATS

Yes, and you know why that's not possible.

FLORENCE

Oh, yes, we mustn't forget the beautiful Maud Gonne. And that you are everlastingly in love with her.

YEATS

In love with her? There have been times when I wished she were dead or I were dead. At least, we'd let each other go.

FLORENCE

You are still very much in love with her.

YEATS

I have never lied to you about that.

FLORENCE

I might be kinder if you had.

YEATS

Would it?

FLORENCE

No, I suppose not. How long will she stay in London this time?

YEATS

I'm not sure. She plans to go to Ireland before she returns to Paris. I certainly can't predict what she'll do.

FLORENCE

She's been very elusive of late.

YEATS

Yes, Maud is nothing if not elusive.

FLORENCE

Not much comfort on a cold night.

YEATS

No, not much comfort on a cold night.

FLORENCE

There's something I've been wanting to give you, and this seems to be that moment.
(She holds out a key.)
The key to my townhouse. When you at last give up your hopeless love, will you remember what I can give you and she cannot?

YEATS

Florence, I'm not sure that I...have anything to give.

FLORENCE

But I know that you have.

YEATS

Do you? Some nights I can't sleep, wanting...I don't know.... I get up and walk half the night.

FLORENCE

I know.

YEATS

Do you?

FLORENCE

Yes, I do. I'm as human as you are.

YEATS

But am I human? Dreams are all I've ever held in my arms for all
these years.

FLORENCE

You need more than dreams.

(SHE puts the key into HIS hand.)

YEATS

(Hesitating, then accepting the key.)
Dreams are all I know.

FLORENCE

The reality is rather more fun.

YEATS

But what is my reality? Florence, my dear, there's something I have
to tell you.

FLORENCE

You needn't tell me. I already know.

YEATS

But I need to tell you. I have spent all these wasted years caught in
a net of dreams. I have never made love to anyone.

FLORENCE

It's all right, my dear. I have.
(SHE walks up to HIM and places his arms around
her.)
It begins like this.

(Slowly SHE begins to kiss HIM, and HE begins
to respond.)

CROWLEY
(Entering DL, clapping.)
Bravo! Most entertaining! Pity to interrupt so tender a scene.

FLORENCE
Oh...!

YEATS
(Erupting.)
What the hell are *you* doing here?

CROWLEY
Surprised to see me?

YEATS
Nothing you do could surprise me!

CROWLEY
You *were* surprised, but *your* touching revelation didn't surprise me in the least.

YEATS
My revelation is none of your damn business!

CROWLEY
(To FLORENCE.)
Ah, Mrs. Emery, as fascinating as ever.

(HE kisses FLORENCE's hand.)

FLORENCE
If you had any manners, Crowley, you would know that in polite society only servants listen at keyholes.

CROWLEY

I've always found polite society to be a crashing bore....
(To YEATS.)
Almost as boring, Yeats, as self-professed poets.

FLORENCE

We thought you were still in Paris.

CROWLEY

As soon as I heard of the initiation tonight and knew that you, my dear, would be here, I came at once. The charms of Paris could no longer keep me away.

YEATS

I am rather fed up with your dubious charms, Crowley. What is the real reason you are here?

CROWLEY

I am a member of The Order of the Golden Dawn. I assume that members attend meetings. Or has Yeats, "our local leader," decided on a membership of one where he leads only himself?

YEATS

If you and Mathers think you can rule our London Temple from Paris, you are both mad.

CROWLEY
(Handing a letter to YEATS.)
From one mad man to another.

YEATS
(Taking the letter, then reading aloud.)
My God! Listen to this. Another directive from our "mad king" in Paris: "I insisted upon your complete and absolute submission to my authority as regards the management of The Order of the Golden Dawn. I am sending Aleister Crowley as my personal emissary with specific instructions which you are to follow to the letter."

(To CROWLEY.)

So—I am to take my orders from the likes of Aleister Crowley. Well, out with it. What specific instructions do you bring?

CROWLEY

Simply that you are to stop initiating members into The Order of the Golden Dawn until further notice.

FLORENCE

But we are initiating Fiona MacLeod tonight. What should we do about that?

CROWLEY

My dear, I don't make the news. I simply report it.

YEATS

If Mathers wants a confrontation, he shall have it. I intend to go to Paris and have it out with him once and for all. In the meantime, Crowley, I am the leader of this Temple. What do you intend to do about it?

CROWLEY

Why should I do anything? I'm sure you will save me the trouble. As a devoted member of The Order of the Golden Dawn, I am here simply to act as an observer.

YEATS

And to act as an informer.

CROWLEY

Why, of course. I wouldn't want to disappoint you.

(There is a sharp KNOCK at the outer door, off R. The KNOCK is repeated, insistently.)

FLORENCE
(Crossing DR, as if looking out a window.)

I can't see who it is.

YEATS

It wouldn't be Stoker. He has a key.

CROWLEY

Whoever it is, I'll get rid of him.
    (HE exits DR. HIS VOICE is heard off.)
My dear fellow, you needn't pound on the door. We're not deaf.

SHARP
    (VOICE off R.)
Don't "dear fellow" me. I understand my cousin, Miss Fiona MacLeod, is expected here tonight.

CROWLEY
    (VOICE off.)
If you're looking for Miss MacLeod, she isn't here.

SHARP
    (VOICE off.)
Do you imagine I would take your word for it? I intend to see for myself.

    (HE appears DR.)

CROWLEY
    (At DR door.)
Be my guest.

    (WILLIAM SHARP enters, very upset. HE is followed leisurely by CROWLEY, who is obviously enjoying the scene.)

SHARP

Forgive my intrusion, Mrs. Emery, Mr. Yeats.

CROWLEY

Don't you want me to forgive your intrusion, Mr. Sharp?

SHARP

I don't believe we've been formally introduced, Mr. Crowley.

CROWLEY

Unless one counts your scathing review of my last book. You tore it to shreds. I would say that's an introduction of sorts.

SHARP

I write only the truth as I see it.

CROWLEY

Yes, as *you* see it. Your vision is rather myopic.

YEATS

We do not encourage visitors, Mr. Sharp. What can we do for you?

SHARP

I'm seeking my cousin, Miss Fiona MacLeod.

YEATS

As you can see, she is not here.

SHARP

I know that you have been in correspondence with her, Mr. Yeats, and that she has been invited to take part in your proceedings. In fact, that she is to be initiated into your order this very night. I cannot and will not allow this to take place.

FLORENCE

Surely Miss MacLeod is an adult and capable of making her own decisions.

SHARP

You must understand me, Mrs. Emery. My cousin is something of a recluse. She is extremely shy and withdrawn. Up until now, she has always trusted my judgment, but lately.... I was quite surprised, I can tell you, that she would consent to join The Order of the Golden Dawn.

CROWLEY

He imagines we intend to use her for our own nefarious purposes.
Wherever would he get such an idea?

FLORENCE

Your sarcasm won't help matters.

YEATS

What is it, Mr. Sharp, that concerns you?

SHARP

Just what is The Order of the Golden Dawn?

YEATS

(Speaking out of whole-hearted commitment—not
pedantically.)
All about us, humans are aware of more than science can explain. Is
this awareness magical?

SHARP

Magical..!?

YEATS

Is it Divine intervention? Or is it the work of the Devil and his Dark
Angels?

CROWLEY

(Crossing away from YEATS in mock fright and ut-
tering a high-pitched, mock-scary sound.)
Wooo! Woo-o-oo!

SHARP

(Increasingly apprehensive.)
The Devil and his Dark Angels?

YEATS

Or is it the work of the human will operating at unexplored depths?

What are these unseen forces—these unexplained links between man and nature? What are these worlds beyond the normal senses? The occult Order of the Golden Dawn, by the invocation of ancient ritual, and the application of joined human wills, intends to find out.

SHARP
(Agitatedly.)
Your discoveries may open doors you cannot close!
(Struggling to restore HIS composure.)
Before I can allow my cousin to become a member of The Golden Dawn, I must determine for myself its suitability for the suggestible mind of a young woman of good family. As a noted critic and scholar, I am willing to substitute myself as a member of your order.

CROWLEY
You are willing to become a member without being invited, I take it.

SHARP
I am submitting my application to Mr. Yeats, not to you, Mr. Crowley. I don't believe you and I have anything in common.

CROWLEY
Don't you? Indeed? Then why would I want you as a member?

SHARP
I don't believe Mr. Yeats will allow you to decide who joins this order.

CROWLEY
And I don't believe even Yeats feels we are in need of a pedantic scribbler, a narrow-minded critic, and a pompous fool!

SHARP
You describe yourself admirably! You are an upstart! A nobody! While *I* have power and influence in London's literary circles!

CROWLEY

Lucky for you since you have no power or influence here.

SHARP

I have this much power. I shall never allow my cousin to be influenced by the likes of Aleister Crowley, or to associate with you in any way!

FLORENCE

Haven't you heard, Mr. Sharp? A new century is dawning, when women as well as men will be completely free from outmoded convention.

CROWLEY

I should hope that Miss MacLeod is capable of deciding for herself what is in her own best interest.

SHARP

How dare you tell be what she is capable of! How dare you even speak her name! You have never met her! You don't know her at all as I do! No one knows her as I do! She needs to be protected from herself, and I intend to do so. I demand to know where she is! Where have you hidden her? I know you are keeping her in hiding!

(HE begins to cross to the double panels UC.)

YEATS
Blocking SHARP's way.)
You can't go in there.

SHARP

How dare you block my way!

YEATS

Look here, Sharp. If I give you my word she is not here, will you believe me?

SHARP

And your word that she is not expected?

YEATS

That I cannot promise.

SHARP

Just as I thought! I shall find her and keep her from coming here, by force if necessary! I shall get a warrant for your arrest, all of you! I shall have you behind bars!

YEATS

On what charges, may I ask?

SHARP

The seduction of a pure and innocent young woman.

FLORENCE

Seduction!

CROWLEY

Charges of seduction before I've even seen her! This is a first.

SHARP

I shall go straight to the police! I promise you that!

CROWLEY

You are the intruder here, Sharp. If you don't quit these premises at once, I won't bother to call the police. I, personally, will throw you out.

SHARP

How dare you! You have not heard the last of this!

> (HE exits in anger, DR, slamming the outer door behind HIM.)

FLORENCE

Well, what do you make of that?

YEATS

I don't know. I've never seen him like that.

CROWLEY

This obsession with the seduction of his cousin—seems he has a few incestuous thoughts of his own.

YEATS

He's certainly being overprotective. I believe he's the last of his family—he and his cousin, that is.

FLORENCE

Overprotective! He was livid with rage. You heard what he said. He threatened to call the police!

CROWLEY

I should have thrown him out on his ear.

YEATS

Yes, your usual subtle approach.

FLORENCE

Willie, the others will be here at any moment. What should we do?

YEATS

We go ahead with the initiation, when I return with Maud.

FLORENCE

Oh, yes, I forgot Miss Gonne. We wouldn't want to keep *her* waiting. You should go at once.

YEATS

Are you sure you'll be all right?

FLORENCE

Oh, Willie, of course I'll be all right. I am the New Woman. I don't need a chaperone.

CROWLEY

Don't worry, Yeats. Mrs. Emery, as you know, is absolutely ravishing tonight, but I shall restrain myself until you return. Wouldn't want you to miss anything.

FLORENCE

Willie, please—go. Bram will be here at any moment.

YEATS

You're sure you'll be all right?

FLORENCE

Of course. Now go, my dear.

(YEATS exits DR.)

CROWLEY

Do I get the impression that you and poor Yeats have not yet become lovers?

FLORENCE

My "lovers" are none of your business.

CROWLEY

If it's virgins you're after, that leaves me out.

FLORENCE

But you were never in.

CROWLEY

And it would seem, my dear, neither were you. I have heard about your rival, the beautiful Maud Gonne, the champion of Ireland, the accomplished actress.

FLORENCE

Actress? So she would like to believe. I suppose it does take acting ability of sorts to advocate revolution while wearing expensive gowns straight from Paris.

CROWLEY

Do I detect a note of jealousy?

FLORENCE

Not at all. I don't choose to be jealous of a marble statue, beautiful but cold. However, there is some rumor of a French liaison which may explain her living so long in Paris.

CROWLEY

How delicious! The human comedy never ceases to amuse. Maud Gonne leaps the channel for love. Yeats sighs over the beautiful Maud. You pant for Yeats, our poet, while I lust after you.

FLORENCE

Oh—lust—yes, how very convenient. What about warmth, tenderness, love?

CROWLEY

Why do women always talk about love when it is lust that loosens your Victorian corsets?

FLORENCE

I suspect you are your own best lover. You don't need us at all.

CROWLEY

You're quite wrong. I consider women a necessity.

FLORENCE

A necessity?

CROWLEY

They should be delivered at the back door each morning with the milk, then carted away with the empty containers.

FLORENCE

Delivered with the milk, indeed! I don't fancy myself an "empty container." At any rate, I don't wish to discuss love or lust with you.

CROWLEY

Actions speak louder than words. Obviously, your poet is all words and no action.

FLORENCE

And perhaps you are all action and no substance.

CROWLEY

Would you care to find out?

FLORENCE

I think not!

CROWLEY

I thought not. But you will.

FLORENCE

You're impossible.

STOKER
(VOICE off.)

Anyone here?

(BRAM STOKER enters. HE is in correct evening dress.)

FLORENCE

Bram, I'm so glad you're here.

STOKER

Ah, my dear, Florence.... Crowley, you here? Up to your old tricks, I see, frightening beautiful women.

CROWLEY

One must stay amused.

STOKER

Florence, you're as beautiful and as charming as ever.

FLORENCE

Thank you, kind sir. How is the show going?

STOKER

We're doing rather well. When will your star brighten our stage again? You must have Shaw write you another play like *Arms and the Man*.

FLORENCE

I'm afraid Bernard Shaw is rather peeved with me just at present. He says I'm not dedicated enough to my craft.

STOKER

No use arguing with Shaw. He has opinions on everything.

CROWLEY

And delivered by his characters in boring detail.

STOKER
(To CROWLEY.)

We weren't expecting you tonight. We thought you were still in Paris.

CROWLEY

And I thought *you* were still in Paris.

STOKER

Paris? No, I wish I were.

CROWLEY

I thought I saw you in Paris some weeks ago in a rather disreputable district. When I tried to call out, you disappeared into the crowd.

STOKER

I am one of those unfortunately bland-looking people who constantly remind one of someone else. No, I've been much too busy at the Lyceum Theatre to have time for an excursion to Paris.

FLORENCE

Bram, we just had the most dreadful scene. William Sharp was here just before you arrived, threatening us with jail and really behaving in a most extraordinary way.

STOKER

Why was he so upset?

CROWLEY

He thinks we are going to seduce his cousin, Miss MacLeod. Sacrificial virgin and all that.

STOKER

How preposterous.

CROWLEY

Speak for yourself.

STOKER

Sharp has always seemed a responsible sort.

FLORENCE

How a poet with Fiona MacLeod's delicate, haunted quality could come from the same family as boring William Sharp is beyond me.

CROWLEY

Have you met the elusive Miss MacLeod?

FLORENCE

No one I know has, but I can hardly wait to meet her.

STOKER

Was Yeats here when Sharp arrived?

FLORENCE

Yes, but Willie left afterwards to pick up Maud. Bram, perhaps you could see Sharp tomorrow and clear up this misunderstanding. We only seek to enhance the artistic vision. We wouldn't hurt a fly.

CROWLEY

My God, that's the trouble! The Order of the Golden Dawn is becoming more like a lady's reading circle every day. All very correct and genteel. Next we'll be serving tea with bread and jam.

STOKER

Just what would you suggest?

CROWLEY

Are we a magical order or not? Then, by Zeus, let's make magic! If we are to accomplish anything, we must be in league with powers larger than ourselves.

STOKER

Do you acknowledge powers larger than yourself, Crowley?

CROWLEY

Yes. The powers of light and darkness. The shadow world—where real monsters appear. The darkness—where your Dracula was born.

STOKER

Oh, my make-believe monster. My pot-boiler Gothic.

CROWLEY

There may be more boiling in that pot than anyone suspects. Perhaps a few genuine skeletons, a severed head or two.

STOKER

I must confess, Crowley, my Dracula was invented as something of a joke. Somehow, he's caught on. I'm really rather amused.

CROWLEY

Are you? I don't think you're nearly as amused as you pretend.

STOKER

Surely I should know whether or not I'm amused by my own joke. I *am* the author, you know, old chap.

CROWLEY

An author seldom understands what he's created. His creation is like a Frankenstein's monster, marauding about the countryside, no longer under the control of its creator. That's your Dracula, Stoker.

STOKER

I'm flattered, Crowley, that you would suggest my poor little joke has become a "creation." Sounds very grand, indeed, but I'm not convinced.

CROWLEY

Your Dracula is a real monster. He will devour you. Wait and see. He'll be impossible to kill.

STOKER

Impossible to kill?

CROWLEY

He'll be alive when you are dead and gone.

STOKER

You are being melodramatic.

CROWLEY

Oh, no, Stoker. You have summoned him, and he has appeared. He'll suck your blood like an incubus.

FLORENCE

Oh, how delightfully scary. You send chills all over me!
(To STOKER.)
I can hardly wait, my dear, to see your monster on the stage. How are the rehearsals going?

STOKER

The usual snags, but that's not what worries me. I'm not at all sure the public will want to see a play about a vampire.

CROWLEY

I know the play-going public: They are panting for that bite in the neck. All that sucking, sucking from the throats of swooning young virgins.

STOKER

Crowley, I suspect that you could create a far more convincing monster than my Dracula.

CROWLEY

I create myself. You project your vampire into a fictional character because you're afraid of the Dracula within. I am not afraid. I intend to *be* the Beast.

FLORENCE

I've often wondered how you got the nickname "Beast." It, of course, suits you.

CROWLEY

My mother gave me the name. She said I reminded her of the Beast out of the Book of Revelations. "You are the Beast from the Bottomless Pit!" she said to me one afternoon over tea. I decided to prove her right. One so hates to make a liar of one's own mother.

FLORENCE

What a charming household.

CROWLEY

She leads a fanatical sect who believe anything if duly recorded in Genesis.

STOKER

Your mother seems to have a great influence on you.

CROWLEY

My father impressed me even more. After a lifetime of quoting scripture, he died of cancer of the tongue.

FLORENCE

How terrible for you.

CROWLEY

No, for him. I was eleven at the time and away at school. I dreamed of his death the night he died and awoke in absolute terror. After that, I was convinced that I had second sight!

FLORENCE

And do you?

CROWLEY

No, for I have often dreamed of my mother's death, only to awaken and find that she is still, unfortunately, alive and preaching.

FLORENCE

Your are outrageous!

STOKER

I suspect Crowley delights in being outrageous. At least one is always "on stage."

CROWLEY

Better than being hypocritical and dull. Those are truly unpardonable sins.

STOKER

On stage, yes, but in real life, hardly.

CROWLEY

In real life? Do you call this "real life?" We are all merely the poses
we assume, the masks we wear. You there, Stoker, pose as a proper
Victorian gentleman while letting loose on the streets of London a
night-stalking vampire.

STOKER

You are being melodramatic!

CROWLEY

Am I? Then how do you explain the series of mysterious disappear-
ances in the past decade, people of both sexes and ages? Only one or
two bodies were ever found. The rest simply vanished.

STOKER

Perhaps they chose to "vanish" for reasons of their own.

FLORENCE

The streets of London are the safest place in the world.

CROWLEY

Are they? Have you ever thought that at this moment Jack the
Ripper is somewhere on the streets of London? He has never been
caught, you know. In fact, one of us could be Jack the Ripper.

FLORENCE

One of us?

CROWLEY

Yes, any one of us could be Jack the Ripper.

STOKER

Now you are being absurd.

CROWLEY

Am I, Stoker? Have you never wanted to bend another human being to your will—to have the power of life and death—to put your mouth to another's throat and taste blood...?

(Sudden SOUND of very loud knocking off, DR.)

FLORENCE
(Startled.)

Oh!

STOKER
(Startled, rises.)

Who's that?

CROWLEY

I'll see.

(HE quickly exits DR.)

STOKER
(Crossing to R.)
Our friend, Crowley, always manages to put my nerves on edge.

FLORENCE

I know just what you mean.

(CROWLEY enters DR with an envelope in HIS hand and glances out the window.)

STOKER

Who was it?

CROWLEY

I don't know. When I opened the door, no one was there. Only this envelope under the door.
(HE takes a note out of the envelope and reads.)

"I am held captive by Shadow. I dream passionate and terrible dreams, my waking dreams aflame. Deep in the dreams of sleep, I cry for release as I sink from gulf to gulf, from darkness into death. Help me! Can I trust you?"

FLORENCE
What does it mean, "I am held captive by Shadow?" It sends shivers over me.

STOKER
"Help me. Can I trust you?"

FLORENCE
It's a cry for help.

STOKER
Don't let it upset you. It's just someone's idea of a prank.
(To CROWLEY.)
Who sent it?

CROWLEY
I don't know. There's no signature.

(HE hands the note to STOKER.)

FLORENCE
Oh, I wish Willie and Maud would get here.

CROWLEY
(Peering DR as if through a window.)
I think your wish has been granted. A hansom cab is just pulling up outside. That leaves you two more wishes. I hope I am included in the second.

FLORENCE
If wishes were horses, we all would ride.

CROWLEY

Just what I had in mind.

(YEATS enters DR.)

FLORENCE

Oh, Willie, I'm so glad you're here.

YEATS
(Shakes hands with STOKER.)

Good to see you, Stoker.

STOKER

Glad you're here. We were becoming concerned.

YEATS

I'm sorry we're late. The fog is so thick you would think we were in the middle of the Channel. Is Miss MacLeod here?

FLORENCE

She hasn't arrived yet. Did you see anyone outside when you drove up?

YEATS

No, no one.

STOKER

Just now, there was a loud knocking at the door. Someone left this note.

(STOKER hands the note to YEATS.)

YEATS
(Reading aloud.)

"I am being held captive by Shadow. I dream passionate and terrible dreams."

CROWLEY

Don't we all?

YEATS

"My waking dreams aflame. Deep in the dreams of sleep I cry for
release as I sink from gulf to gulf, from darkness into death. Help
me! Can I trust you?"

FLORENCE

It's a cry for help.

YEATS

It's from Fiona MacLeod.

FLORENCE

Fiona MacLeod?

YEATS

Yes. I recognize her handwriting.

FLORENCE

Does it mean that she is actually held captive?

STOKER

Or is it just an expression?

CROWLEY

Our mystery woman is becoming more interesting by the moment.

STOKER

You recognize her handwriting, Yeats. What do you know of her?

YEATS

I've never met her. I have corresponded with her over a period of
time. This note is authentic both as to her handwriting and her

manner of expression. I hope she has not been frightened away. I hope she can trust us.

FLORENCE

What should we do...? We must do something.

YEATS

Let's not overreact.
> (Crosses DR and calls off.)

For God's sake, Maud. What are you doing out there? Do come in. Everyone is here by Miss MacLeod.

MAUD

> (VOICE off.)

I'm coming. Don't be so impatient, Willie.
> (MAUD enters, pausing to make an "entrance.")

Willie, you promised me you'd keep copies of *The United Irishman* on the hall table.

YEATS

I've been putting them there.

MAUD

Well, they are not there now! Arthur Griffith has been reprinting my articles from *L'Irelande Libre*—and I want them to be read in London!

YEATS

Maud, I have been putting copies of *The United Irishman* out there every week! I can't watch over them like a mother hen!

MAUD

No, you can't! You are very near-sighted.

YEATS

You know Mrs. Emery, of course.

MAUD

Of course. How are you, Mrs. Emery?

FLORENCE

Well, thank you. So good to see you, Miss Gonne.

MAUD

So good to see you again, Mrs. Emery.
(To STOKER.)
Bram, so good to see you again.

STOKER

My dear, it's been much too long. You're just over from Paris, I hear.
How long can you stay this time?

MAUD

I don't know. It all depends on the situation in Ireland.

STOKER

I don't believe you've met Aleister Crowley—a new member of our
Order. He was initiated at Mark Masons Hall. Aleister Crowley,
Miss Maud Gonne.

MAUD
(Giving CROWLEY HER hand.)
How do you do.

CROWLEY
(Taking HER hand but not releasing it.)
You are the most beautiful woman I've ever met.

MAUD

That is very flattering.

CROWLEY
(Dropping HER hand.)
Not at all. I dislike beautiful women.

MAUD

Oh? And why is that?

CROWLEY

They seldom have any imagination and are usually very dull. Are you very dull?

MAUD

Only on Thursdays when I am at home. You must catch me earlier in the week.

STOKER

Don't mind him, my dear. Crowley is in a crusading mood, against the unpardonable sin of dullness.

FLORENCE

He would have all of us dull folk stood up against the wall and shot.

MAUD

Do you have enough blindfolds?

CROWLEY

Since most of England is already blind, that won't be necessary.

MAUD

I must agree with you there. Our only hope is Ireland.

CROWLEY

Ireland? Hope? A sign should be posted at every Irish port of entry: "Abandon hope all you who enter here!"

YEATS

Now that Crowley has demolished both England and Ireland without firing a shot, we have other matters to discuss. We've had a strange note from Miss MacLeod. Here, read it for yourself.

MAUD
(Takes the note and reads silently.)
But I don't understand. What does this mean?

YEATS
I don't know. She may have changed her mind about the initiation.
She seems deeply troubled.

MAUD
Oh, this is too much! Do you mean I came all the way from Paris
for nothing? Mathers sends that insufferable letter ordering us not
to have an initiation and now this. I did not join this Order to be
ordered about.

CROWLEY
Why did you join The Order of the Golden Dawn, Miss Gonne?

MAUD
I thought we were all artists and free thinkers. Not hopelessly involved with middle-class notions of position. I thought, of course,
the Order would be for Irish Independence. I certainly didn't join
the Order to chase illusions.

YEATS
But don't you see, all civilization is held together by illusion, like
the suggestions of an invisible hypnotist. Poetry and myth are the
only true reality. They weave all the material world together with the
shuttle of illusion.

MAUD
I prefer to live in the real world, if you don't mind.

YEATS
Where is the reality of music? Each note vanishes into thin air even
as it is being played. We are all the masks we wear, the parts we play,
but what shadows lie behind our masks?

MAUD

You are beginning to make my head ache. All this talk of what is real and not real. I am not interested. I am only interested in whether I serve the cause of Ireland. What does a mask have to do with that?

YEATS

I has everything to do with that. How many men will believe your beauty is Ireland—and die as a result?

MAUD

What better death than to die for Beauty and for Ireland?

YEATS

Better to live—for Beauty and for Ireland.
                   (To the OTHERS.)
This is an old argument between Miss Gonne and myself. She thinks dynamite and death will build a better world.

MAUD

And Willie thinks poetry will feed the hungry masses.

YEATS

Man cannot live by bread alone.

MAUD

             (Rising, becoming the rousing orator.)
Tell that to those who starved in the Great Irish Famine and are still starving. Men and women ate the dogs, the rats, and the grass of the fields. Whole families, when they knew they had to die, closed up the doors of their cabins with stones, that no one might look upon their last agony. Oh, Willie, don't talk to me of poetry while there is still hunger in Ireland.

YEATS

Do you think Ireland is the only place where there is hunger? They you've never walked the slums of Seven Dials and Whitechapel as I have. The poor in London are as destitute and desperate as any peasant in Ireland. Why can't your compassion go out to them?

MAUD

My heart is in Ireland.

FLORENCE

At least in London there are theatres and restaurants.

CROWLEY

There speaks the actress—theatres and restaurants! Let them eat cake!

STOKER
(Looking out DR as if through a window.)
There's a hansom cab stopping just outside. A woman is being handed down by the driver. I think our new member has arrived after all.

YEATS

I'll go out and bring her in. Let me tell her about Sharp.

(YEATS exits DR.)

CROWLEY

I can hardly wait to see beneath that veil.

MAUD

I thought you didn't like beautiful women, Mr. Crowley.

CROWLEY

In your case, I'm willing to make an exception.

MAUD

How very generous.

YEATS
(Entering.)
May I present the famous poet of the Celtic twilight, Miss Fiona
MacLeod.

(Delicately and hesitantly, FIONA MacLEOD
enters DR. SHE is dressed in a long black dress,
a short black cape, and black gloves. A black lace
veil entirely covers HER face and head and falls to
HER shoulders. The face behind the veil is hidden.
SHE gives the impression of mystery and grace, of
hidden beauty.

May I present our company. Miss Maud Gonne and Mrs. Florence
Farr Emery.

MAUD
We are so pleased to have you with us.

FLORENCE
I have so wanted to meet you.

FIONA
(Bowing HER head delicately and shyly.)
Thank you.

YEATS
Mr. Bram Stoker, the noted author and manager of the Lyceum
Theatre.

STOKER
I am honored, Miss. MacLeod.

YEATS
And Mr. Aleister Crowley, sometime mountain climber and magus.
It is his own designation.

CROWLEY
I see you have already met Mr. William Butler Yeats, sometime

poet. It is his own designation. Will you allow me to help you with your veil?

(HE starts to reach toward HER.)

FIONA
(Drawing back in fright.)
Oh, no—please—don't. Oh—I'm sorry—forgive me. Forgive me for being—the way I am. I don't go about in society very much.

YEATS
We received your note. We were afraid you might not come.

FIONA
I, too, was afraid I would not have the courage. If my cousin, William Sharp, were only here—he has always acted for me in the world.

YEATS
Your cousin was here, Miss MacLeod. He created something of a scene. He is very opposed to your joining our Order.

FIONA
I—I knew he would object.

YEATS
You are free to go or stay, just as you please. If you stay, it must be of your own free will. Do you understand?

FIONA
Yes—I understand.

YEATS
It is my duty to warn you, Miss MacLeod. This initiation cannot be taken lightly. We believe that whatever is manifest in the material world first appears in the world of our imagination. With this initiation, you open a door you may never be able to close.

FIONA

If I go now—I will never again have the courage to face the world. This is my last hope to be free. Do you understand?

YEATS

Yes, I do. You have the soul of a poet will imprisoned in its chrysalis. You want to spread your iridescent wings and fly in the sun.

FIONA

Yes, oh yes! I knew you would understand. You of all people would understand.

YEATS

We hope to form a crucible for a new knowledge which will lift man's spirit from darkness into light. Do you wish to join our quest?

FIONA

Yes. It is my one last hope—for freedom and for joy. I want to join—if you will have me.

MAUD

Of course. We want you to stay.

FLORENCE

Yes, you are one of us. We are all artists here.

STOKER

You are safe here with us, Miss MacLeod.

CROWLEY

And now that your are to be one of us—your veil.

(HE reaches as if to lift the veil.)

FIONA

But—must I remove my veil?

YEATS

Not if you don't want to. As part of our ritual, we all wear masks that conceal *and* reveal our true identities.

FIONA

You are—very kind.

YEATS

If you will go with Miss Gonne and Mrs. Emery to put on your robes and masks, the ritual of initiation can begin. They will tell you what to do.

FLORENCE

Come, my dear. There is an Oriental screen in the next room. If you like, you can put on your robe and mask behind the screen.

FIONA

Thank you. I should like that.

(MAUD, FLORENCE, and FIONA exit DL. YEATS, STOKER, and CROWLEY move the furniture to the side walls. THEY cross UC and open the large, double-hinged panels which form the back wall of the room. THEY light the candles on the altar and turn down the gaslight in the main room. YEATS, STOKER, and CROWLEY exit R. YEATS reenters in a long black robe and mask. YEATS stands in front of the altar. HE strikes the bell three times then turns to face the audience. At the sound of the bell, CROWLEY and STOKER, in long black robes and masks, enter R in procession as MAUD and FLORENCE, in long black robes and masks, enter L in simultaneous procession. THEY position themselves in a triangle, YEATS before the altar at the apex, MAUD and STOKER at R, FLORENCE and CROWLEY at L. YEATS strikes the bell three times, and FIONA enters L. FIONA is wearing a

gray robe with a gray veil covering HER head and
falling to HER shoulders. The veil completely hides
FIONA's facial features. FIONA crosses to stand before YEATS. MAUD reacts to FIONA's appearance
in sudden fright.)

YEATS

We call on the spirit of the New Age to be present in this room, to
lead and guide us into Light.... Child of Earth, why do you seek to
enter our sacred hall?

FIONA

My soul wanders in darkness and seeks the light of hidden knowledge.

YEATS

That light shall be revealed.
                    (YEATS picks up a sword from the altar, and FIO-
                    NA kneels before HIM. YEATS touches HER head
                    with the sword.)
Do you further promise and swear that from this day forward you
will not abuse the great power entrusted in you?

FIONA

I swear.

YEATS

And if you break this, your magical obligation, you will submit
yourself, by your own consent, to a deadly and hostile current of
will set in motion by the Secret Chiefs of this Order, by which you
might be slain as by your own hand. Do you solemnly swear?

FIONA

I solemnly swear.

YEATS

(Turning the sword so that the point is above FIO-
NA's head, HE touches HER on both shoulders as
HE recites.)

Child of Earth, long hast thou dwelt in darkness. Quit the night,
and seek the day.

(HE returns the sword to the altar. HE holds out
HIS hand and takes FIONA's hand.)

Arise, Child of Earth. We receive thee into the Golden Dawn.

(HE moves away, leaving FIONA alone at the altar.)

ALL (Except CROWLEY)

We receive thee into the Golden Dawn.

YEATS

The ceremony is at an end. Go now, and live in the light of the
Golden Dawn.

(Removing their masks, MAUD and FLORENCE
cross to FIONA.)

MAUD

Congratulations, Miss MacLeod. We are so happy to have you with us.

FLORENCE

We are really very pleased that you are now one of us.

CROWLEY

I cannot believe what I am hearing!

(Mocking the women.)

"So happy to have you with us." "Really very pleased that you are
one of us." Your tea chatter makes me want to vomit!

YEATS
(Removing HIS mask.)
I have had enough of your cynical mockery and your foul mouth! If you don't like this ritual, get out!

CROWLEY
Do call this revolting display of Victorian snobbery a "ritual"—this mockery of empty words masquerading as magic?

STOKER
(Having removed HIS mask.)
Now look here, Crowley...!

CROWLEY
No! You look here! Magic demands blood and passion and fire—human sacrifice and the will to make it happen!

(HE grabs the sword from the altar.)

YEATS

Put that down!

CROWLEY
(Pointing the sword at YEATS.)
Stand back!

YEATS

What do you think you're doing?

CROWLEY
I know what I'm doing, Yeats, because I know who I am. I am not a faint-hearted, failed poet playing at fantasy. I know what I want, and I have the will, the passion, and the fire to make it happen. You have asked for magic! You shall have it! All we need is blood!
(Holding the sword high, intoning.)
I call on the Demon of the Abyss, coupling shape of beast and man, come forth! Accept this sacrifice of passion, blood, and fire!

(HE cuts HIS hand with the sword, and blood flows from the wound.)

Manifest to me!

(The stage suddenly darkens, and there is a SOUND as of a distant rumble of thunder. The door DR blows open, and a wind causes the candles and the gaslights to flicker, throwing grotesque shadows across the wall. One giant shadow seems to move across the stage.)

MAUD

Oh—what is it?

FLORENCE

It's so cold!

MAUD

Like a breath from the grave.

STOKER

Something's entered this room!

YEATS

Who is it? Who is there?

FIONA
(Now speaking in a deep, eerie voice.)
You thought to keep me out, but I have entered. I am here.

MAUD and FLORENCE

Oh!

YEATS

Who—are you?

FIONA
(Deep, eerie voice.)
One who has come from darkness into light.

FLORENCE
Whose voice is that?

STOKER
She's in a trance.

FIONA
(Deep, eerie voice.)
I see your past lives played out before my inner vision.
(SHE turns to YEATS and MAUD.)
I see a man and a woman. That same man and woman who are here
in this room.
(YEATS and MAUD move forward as if entranced.)
I see a medieval knight, vowed to celibacy, who loved his sister with
an unholy love. He builds a great stone cross and spends his days
standing against it...
(YEATS mimes the words that follow, arms outstretched as if on a cross.)
...with arms outstretched in penance for his sins. Ah-h-h.... One
wishes to speak to the woman who stands beside him.

MAUD
No!

(ALL evidence feeling the power now in the room.
No one is acting naturally.)

FIONA
(Deep, eerie voice.)
A child is here.

MAUD

No! Don't let her speak!

CROWLEY

Don't awaken her! It might be dangerous!

FIONA

(Deep, eerie voice.)

He has come a long way. He is small and fair. He is holding out his hands. He wishes to speak to one here.

MAUD

Oh, my God!

FIONA

(In a child's voice.)

"Mother! Do not cry any more. I am happy now."

MAUD

What else does he say?

FIONA

(Deep, eerie voice.)

Only his name.

MAUD

What is the child's name?

FIONA

(Deep, eerie voice.)

His name is—Georges.

MAUD

Oh...!

(SHE suddenly faints. YEATS and FLORENCE rush to keel by MAUD.)

CROWLEY

Don't anyone move! Can't you feel the dark power in this room?

FIONA

(Turning to CROWLEY, speaking in a deep, eerie voice.

I see a man dressed in a black robe—many centuries ago.

(As FIONA speaks, CROWLEY, as if entranced, mimes the words.)

From a vessel over a fire, he lifts the image of a human form. Its limbs move, and it becomes alive. He has created life and endowed it with an evil spirit. He looks into its eyes as if they were your own.... I see...ah!

(Now in revulsion.)

All degradation...all sheer infamy...thou shalt endure....

CROWLEY

(Drawn into the trance and joining in without pause.)

Thy head beneath the mire and dung shall desire, as in some hateful dream, at last, to lie....

FIONA

(Deep, eerie voice.)

They shall trample thee.

Till thou respire and meet thy doom.

CROWLEY

The vilest worm must crawl.

The loathliest vampire gloom....

STOKER

Crowley! For God's sake!

FIONA

(Now pointing at STOKER and speaking in a deep, eerie voice.)

I see a dark shadow of unspeakable deeds out of the dark shadow of endless time.

STOKER
(Entranced, seeing the same vision.)
I see—maggots feeding on tortured flesh....

FIONA
(Deep, eerie voice.)
A monster of plague and death rising from the corpse....

STOKER
(Seeing the vision.)
Holding out its hands—crawling with maggots...! No! No! Enough!

(STOKER crosses toward FIONA threateningly. CROWLEY intervenes; whereupon, STOKER viciously attacks CROWLEY.)

YEATS
(Hurriedly crossing to CROWLEY and STOKER.)
For God's sake! Stop! Stop, I tell you!
(YEATS separates CROWLEY and STOKER. Staggering to one side, STOKER struggles to regain HIS composure.)
Turn up the lights!
(CROWLEY crosses to a gas light and turns it up. HE takes out a handkerchief and wraps it around HIS bleeding hand. YEATS turns to FIONA.)
Miss MacLeod! Wake up! Wake up!

FIONA
(Now speaking in HER feminine voice.)
Where—where am I?

YEATS

Are you all right?

FIONA

My head is aching so!

STOKER

Did you see it? For God's sake, Yeats! Did you see it? Did you see...?

YEATS

Get a grip on yourself, Stoker!
                (YEATS crosses to MAUD and kneels by HER side.)
Maud! Maud!

                (STOKER, as if to throw off the remnants of HIS
                trance state, pulls off HIS robe and hurls it away,
                then sits distractedly on a side chair.)

FLORENCE

She's coming to.

MAUD

Is he—gone?

YEATS

Are you all right?

MAUD
                (Now sitting up.)
He *is*—gone?

FIONA

My head! What happened?

CROWLEY

You went into a trance. Has that ever happened to you before?

FIONA

I—don't know. I don't know.

CROWLEY

Let me help you.

FIONA

No.... No.... I—wish to be by myself for a moment.

CROWLEY

I shall be happy to escort you home, Miss MacLeod.

FIONA

No—I—would not wish to take you out of your way.

CROWLEY

I can assure you, it's just the direction I intend to go.

YEATS

You aren't going anywhere with her.

CROWLEY

And who's going to stop me?

YEATS

I will. I intend to see that she gets safely home.

CROWLEY

She would be "safe" with you—wouldn't she, Yeats?

YEATS

Better safe with me than in your power.

CROWLEY

You know nothing of the power in this room tonight. I know how to help her, and you do not.

YEATS

She doesn't need your kind of help.

CROWLEY

She is free to decide for herself.

FIONA

No! No! I will never be free! Never!

(SHE abruptly flees, exiting DR.)

YEATS

Miss MacLeod! Wait!

(YEATS starts after her.)

CROWLEY

(Intervening.)

Leave her alone! I warn you!

(CROWLEY exits DR. YEATS starts after HIM.
BOTH have thrown off THEIR robes.)

MAUD

Willie! Don't go!

YEATS

(Turning back.)

Are you all right?

MAUD

Oh, let them go! Let them go!

YEATS

(To FLORENCE.)

Look after her. I've got to find Miss MacLeod. My God, have we all
gone mad?

(HE exits DR.)

MAUD

What happened—when I fainted?

FLORENCE

The mad scene from *MacBeth*, complete with witch's spell and "out, out damned spot." To tell the truth, I don't know what happened.

MAUD

I don't know what came over me. I don't know why I fainted.

FLORENCE

Don't you? You did it very skillfully, just in time to keep Miss MacLeod, or whoever it was, from revealing anything more about you—your affairs.

MAUD

What are you implying?

FLORENCE

I'm not *implying* anything. I'm congratulating you on a scene well played. I know why you fainted and why you don't choose to tell Willie the truth.

MAUD

What do you mean?

FLORENCE

Just what I said.

> (FLORENCE begins to gather up the robes and masks after removing HER own robe.)

MAUD

And will you choose to tell him?

(MAUD removes HER robe and hands it to FLOR-ENCE.)

FLORENCE

No. I wouldn't hurt him that much.

MAUD

Even if it gave you an advantage?

FLORENCE

(Continuing to gather up the discarded robes and masks.)

He would not see it that way.

(Carrying the robes and masks, SHE exits DL. YEATS enters DR.)

YEATS

I can't find either of them. They've vanished into the fog.
(To MAUD.)
You are still very pale. Do you want to rest here a while?

MAUD

Yes. I'm—so cold!

(SHE sits on the sofa.)

YEATS

I'll light a fire.
(Turning to the still-recovering STOKER.)
Are you all right, Stoker?

STOKER

I'm all right—now.
(FLORENCE reenters with HER cloak, gloves, and reticule.)
Miss Emery, may I drop you on my way?

FLORENCE

Yes, thank you.

YEATS

Good night.

FLORENCE

Good night.

STOKER

Good night.

(FLORENCE and STOKER exit DR. YEATS closes the Inner Vault panels then joins MAUD at the sofa, standing before HER, taking HER hands in HIS.)

YEATS

How are you feeling now, my dear? Your hands are so cold. And you are still very pale.

MAUD

I—I'm just tired.

YEATS

And—you're shivering...! I'll light the fire.
                    (HE crosses to the fireplace and lights it.)
That damn Crowley! Playing warlock and using us as his witch's coven! I'll get rid of him if it's the last thing I do. But first, I've got to find out what really happened tonight.

MAUD

What do *you* think—happened?

YEATS

I don't know. There was a power in this room. I know it. I could feel it. I've got to find out what it was.

MAUD

Oh, Willie! Leave it alone! Leave it alone! I'm afraid! Afraid!

YEATS

Maud, what are you afraid of? Tell me, what's troubling you?

MAUD

Oh, Willie, leave me alone! Leave me alone! You aren't my Father Confessor!

YEATS

Do you need one?

MAUD

Don't we all—need one...? Oh, Willie, let's not quarrel. Why are we always quarreling? Let's not quarrel. Not tonight.

YEATS

No, not tonight.
> (Reflectively, YEATS crosses away from MAUD then turns to look at HER.)

My God, you are beautiful! When I look at you, I see the spirit of Ireland—beautiful, proud, and free.... Do you remember that day on the cliffs in Ireland, overlooking the sea?

MAUD

Yes. It was our single perfect day.

YEATS

The old woman in the cottage—she thought we had just been married.

MAUD

Yes, I remember.

YEATS

She called to us, "Joy on your wedding day!"

MAUD

I have never been so happy as I was that day.

YEATS

And I have never been so happy.

MAUD

I wish we could go back. I wish we were there now.

YEATS

We are there. Listen! I can hear the lonely cry of the gulls...!
            (Looking into the fire.)
Look, in the fire—the sailboat beating against the wind, its white
wings floating on the breast of the sea....

MAUD

            (Also looking into the fire.)
And Queen Maeve...
            (Pronounced "Mav.")
...and her warriors riding on the wind. And Aengus...
            (Pronounced "An'-gus.")
...her consort, calling to her through the flames...

YEATS

...And just there, our Castle of Heroes, like the Phoenix, rising from
the ashes!

MAUD

Our Castle of Heroes! Our Golden Dawn...! All our dreams—will
we ever build our Castle of Heroes?

YEATS

Yes, we will build it in the human heart, and young men and wom-
en will be initiated into our mysteries and learn to be as brave as
Cuchulain....
            (Pronounced "Koo-hoo'-lan.")
...and as steadfast as Maeve.

MAUD

Will you ever give up on your dreams?

YEATS

We shall never give up on our dreams as long as we live....
    We shall walk upon long dapple grass
    And pluck 'til time and time are done,
    The silver apples of the moon,
    The golden apples of the sun.

MAUD

I wish we were still there on the cliffs overlooking the sea. That day was like a single, perfect rose—that passes away.

YEATS

    Who dreamed that beauty passes like a dream...?
    We and the labouring world are passing by:
    Amid men's souls, that waver and give place
    Like pale waters in the wintry race,
    Under passing stars, foam of the sky,
    Lives on this lonely face.

MAUD

    Who dreamed that beauty passes like a dream...?
    (Pause.)
I have had dreams of our being together—long, long ago. We were brother and sister in another life. I was a temple priestess, and I betrayed my trust. A child was born, and I killed it to hide my deed.
    (Pause.)
Afterwards, they turned me out into the desert, and you, my brother, chose to go with me. We wandered over burning sands, searching, searching for water to cool our thirst. When I could not go any farther, you held me in your arms and promised never to leave until I died.

YEATS

There may have been times when I wanted you dead and all the searching over.

MAUD

Why must we live it over again?

YEATS

It must all be lived again and again until we learn to love.

MAUD

Promise that you will never leave me until I die. No matter what happens—if I should love someone else, or if you should love someone else—promise that your spirit will never leave mine until I die.

YEATS

I promise that my spirit will never leave yours until I die.

MAUD

Then, whatever happens, it's all right. The world won't understand the love we have for each other. I know that you are my brother, my love, the other half of my soul. If I know that your spirit is with me, whatever comes, then all is well.

YEATS

My spirit is with you, whatever comes.
          (After a contemplative pause.)
I shall always remember this moment—when I loved you with all my heart...! For the hundredth time: Will you marry me?

MAUD

And for the hundredth time: No.

YEATS

Then send me away!

MAUD

Would you go?

YEATS

Would you send me away?

MAUD

I don't have the courage. I need you too much. I need you so now. There's no one else I can turn to—I'm in such anguish.

YEATS

What is it? Tell me...! Your face is still pale. Your hands are so cold...!

(HE takes HER hands in HIS.)

Let me warm them.... Tell me what's troubling you?

MAUD

Do you remember my telling you of my recurring dream that terrifies me so?

YEATS

Of the woman in gray...?

MAUD

Yes—the woman in the gray veil coming out of a gray fog—just like Fiona MacLeod did tonight. Tonight, I saw my dream come to life. Fiona MacLeod is the woman in the gray veil.

YEATS

Then the dream never need terrify you again. You've lived it now.

MAUD

No, that's not all. In my dream, I cannot move. I cannot run away. She accuses me, in a past life, of being the murderer of children.

YEATS

If your were a murderer in a past life, that is why you are alive now—we both believe that. To expiate the karma of the past by our deeds in this life.

MAUD

Oh, but if that is true...if that is true—oh, my God!

YEATS

What is it? Tell me, my dear.

MAUD

Promise that will not hate me for long.

YEATS

I could never hate....

MAUD
(Putting HER hand on HIS lips.)

Sh-h-h. Promise.

YEATS

I promise.

MAUD

Then turn around. You mustn't look at me.
(YEATS turns away.)
Tonight, the woman in gray spoke of a child. His name was—
Georges. That was the name of my son. His father was my lover in
Paris.
(YEATS stiffens.)
No, don't move. Don't turn around. Let me finish what I have to say
while I still have the courage to say it. My son is—dead. He was just
a baby. I left him with nurses in France while I traveled to England
and Ireland for the Irish cause. He got meningitis while I was away.
They could do nothing to save him. I rushed back to Paris, but he
died in my arms. I feel—that I left him when he needed me. I killed
him. Now you know. You can hate me now.
(YEATS does not move or speak, as if HE is
stunned.)
Say something!

YEATS

What do you want me to say?

MAUD

Say something to comfort me!

YEATS

(Bitterly.)

Comfort, is it? You want me to comfort you? Is this comfort enough? Do you kill everything that loves you?

MAUD

(As if HE has struck HER.)

How could you!

YEATS

How could you?

MAUD

My heart is breaking!

YEATS

And you have broken mine!

MAUD

I am in anguish!

YEATS

Does it help that there are two of us? Take comfort in that!

MAUD

Hate me, then! I want you to suffer, too! You are the only one who can share my pain!

(Suddenly, desperately, THEY hold each other, overwhelmed by shared grief.)

YEATS

You must tell me everything, now. Who is he?

MAUD

No one you know. His name is Lucien Millevoye.
(Pronounced "Lu-see-en Mel-vwä.")

YEATS

Why haven't you married him?

MAUD

He has a wife and children. I never meant to marry him.

YEATS

Are you in love with him?

MAUD

No. I don't think I ever was.

YEATS

Have you left him?

MAUD

No.

YEATS

Why do you stay with him—after what has happened?

MAUD

Because of what has happened.

YEATS

What does that mean?

MAUD

You once said that the soul of a dead child can return to a couple in
the birth of a new child. Do you still believe that?

YEATS

Yes. But you can't play dice with human souls.

MAUD

I have to try.

YEATS

Maud, your child is in the hands of God. He is safe now. If Fiona MacLeod speaks true, he came to tell you that himself.

MAUD

If she speaks true. I'm afraid of her. Afraid of what she will mean to all of us. What she has already meant. My dream of the woman in gray—it was always a vision of terror, destroying everything I love.

YEATS

Yes—destroying everything I love. I have been faithful to you all these years. Do you know that?

MAUD

Yes. I told you to take a lover.

YEATS

But you didn't mean it.

MAUD

No, I didn't mean it. I didn't want you to be with someone else.

YEATS

Even while you were.

MAUD

Yes, even then. Will you ever forgive me?

YEATS

No. I don't think I will ever forgive you.

MAUD

Please don't go away in anger.

YEATS

What do you expect? You refuse me, you give yourself to another lover, you have his child—and you ask if I can forgive you?

>   (Taking from HIS pocket the key that FLORENCE
>   had given HIM and tossing it in HIS hand.)

Someone once said to me, "When you last give up your hopeless love, will you remember what I can give you, and she cannot?" And she handed me this key. I will take comfort in that.

>   (YEATS exits R.)

MAUD

>   (Calling after HIM.)

Willie! Don't go like this...!

>   (MAUD turns toward stage left, despondent, HER
>   back to door R. FIONA enters quietly DR, unseen
>   by MAUD. FIONA stares uncertainly at MAUD,
>   who instinctively becomes aware of FIONA's pres-
>   ence. With heightening apprehension, MAUD turns
>   and stares at FIONA. FIONA stares back. MAUD
>   slowly crosses upstage toward the Inner Vault as
>   FIONA crosses to downstage center. MAUD seems
>   to be surrendering to a hypnotic spell originating
>   with FIONA. THEY move in a counter-clockwise,
>   circular motion, FIONA stalking MAUD.)

MAUD

>   (Finally, in terror, forcing HERSELF to speak.)

Who—are—you?

FIONA

Yes. Who am I?

>   (THEY stare at one another for a moment longer,
>   then MAUD escapes, exiting DR.)

SLOW FADE TO BLACK

END OF ACT I

ACT II: SCENE ONE

(It is the following afternoon, about 4 PM in FLOR-ENCE's Egyptian motif sitting room, which is minimally suggested. Tea service is ready on the low table before the sofa. FLORENCE appears to be waiting for someone. SHE is in deep thought and A bit concerned. There is a knock at the door. FLOR-ENCE crosses to the door and opens it. MAUD is there.)

FLORENCE

Won't you come in?

MAUD

Thank you.

(MAUD enters. The two WOMEN are stiff and formal toward each other.)

FLORENCE

I trust you are feeling better?

MAUD

I'm afraid not.

FLORENCE

I'm very sorry.

MAUD

It was good of you to receive me.

FLORENCE

May I take your things?

MAUD

Thank you.

(FLORENCE takes MAUD's cape and places it on a chair by the door. MAUD removes HER gloves but not HER hat. SHE continues to carry HER reticule.)

FLORENCE

Will you have tea?

MAUD

That is very kind of you.

FLORENCE

Not at all. Won't you sit down?
(MAUD sits, as does FLORENCE. FLORENCE pours MAUD's tea.)
Sugar? Cream?

MAUD

No, thank you.
(THEY sip THEIR tea as MAUD glances around the room.)
This is a lovely room. Very exotic. Very Egyptian.

FLORENCE

Do you like it?

MAUD

Very much.

FLORENCE

I'm drawn to all things Egyptian. I believe I lived in Egypt in a previous incarnation.

MAUD

What a coincidence. So did I. Who were you?

FLORENCE

A member of the Pharaoh's court. I may have been poisoned. And you?

MAUD

I was a temple priestess. They turned me out into the desert.

FLORENCE

Interesting. What is your astrological sign?

MAUD

I was born on the cusp between Sagittarius and Capricorn.

FLORENCE

Oh? That explains a good deal.

MAUD

Yes, I daresay it does. I had a purpose in requesting our meeting. May I come straight to the point?

FLORENCE

Yes. That would be best.

MAUD

I think you are in love with Willie.

FLORENCE

Do you? He has been in love with you for a long time.

MAUD

Yes, I know.

FLORENCE

Any you?

MAUD

If I could really be in love with any man, it would be with Willie.

FLORENCE

They why haven't you become lovers?

MAUD

I came to ask you to become his lover.

FLORENCE

You want me to become his lover?

MAUD

Are you shocked?

FLORENCE

No. I don't think "shocked" is the word.

MAUD

What is, then?

FLORENCE

Irony. The irony of the timing, I think.

MAUD

The irony of the timing?

FLORENCE

Yes. Something an actress learns. It's the timing, you see, that makes
a scene either tragic or comic.

MAUD

And our timing?

FLORENCE

Comic. You are a trifle late. Willie and I became lovers last night,
just after he left you.

MAUD

Oh!

FLORENCE

Are *you* shocked?

MAUD

No. I don't think "shocked" is the word.

FLORENCE

What is, then?

MAUD

Irony. The irony of the timing.... I see I needn't have come.

FLORENCE

Just so. Will you take more tea before you go?

MAUD

No, thank you.

FLORENCE

Shall we stop this charade? You say you came to ask me to become Willie's lover. I don't think that you are pleased to find that I have.

MAUD

No, I can't pretend that I am pleased.

FLORENCE

Then charity wasn't your motive in give him to me. You want to depend on his love and give nothing in return.

MAUD

I depend on his love more than I have realized. He and I are two halves of the same soul.

FLORENCE

We are playing comedy indeed. You want Willie's love while you have another man's child.

MAUD

Nothing can change what Willie and I are to each other.

FLORENCE

(Stung to anger.)

Last night he made love to me with all the passion he was never allowed to experience with you. Long after—when I awoke—I saw him lying there sleepless, staring into the dark. So you see, you have nothing to fear. You have given me his body and have kept his soul. How convenient for you.

MAUD

(Rising.)

If it is so convenient for me, why do I feel the way I do?

(MAUD cross to the chair and picks up HER cape. SHE carefully adjusts HER cape and hat in a mirror by the door and slowly draws on HER gloves.)

FLORENCE

You are a very beautiful woman. You can have any woman's lover you desire.

MAUD

(Studying HER reflection in the mirror.)

Yes, I know. Thank you for having me to tea. Please don't bother to see me out.

(SHE exits.)

BLACKOUT

END OF SCENE ONE

ACT II: SCENE TWO

(It is a few hours after Scene One. The meeting
room of The Golden Dawn. The double panels to
the Inner Vault are closed. CROWLEY enters DR.
HE is dressed in evening attire and carrying a bottle
of wine. HE looks around the room then goes to
the side cabinet and takes out two glasses, putting
the bottle and glasses on a tray. HE lights two sets of
candelabra and then goes to the gas lights and turns
them down. A KNOCK is heard off. HE checks the
room, goes to the window DR, and looks out, then
exits DR. FIONA enters DR, followed by CROW-
LEY. FIONA is dressed in the same long, black
dress, black gloves, and black veil covering HER
face and head. Again SHE seems mysterious, ethe-
real, concealing an enigmatic beauty.)

FIONA
(Softly.)
The others? They are not here yet?

CROWLEY
No. Not yet. Do come in. Sit here on the sofa.

(FIONA sits. SHE does not take off her veil or
gloves. CROWLEY crosses to the cabinet and opens
the bottle of wine.)

FIONA
I received a note from Mr. Yeats. He spoke of an unscheduled meeting of The Order of the Golden Dawn.

CROWLEY
(Pouring the wine into two glasses.)
Yes. Totally unexpected. You like your wine dry, I hope. This is really
a very good year.

FIONA

I—don't know. I am not used to drinking wine.

CROWLEY

Oh? What do you prefer?

FIONA

I—am not used to drinking anything.

CROWLEY

Well then, a little wine will be just the thing.
> (Carrying the two glasses, HE crosses to the sofa.
> HE hands a glass to HER and sits beside HER on
> the sofa.)

To our friendship.
> (HE raises his glass and then sips HIS wine while
> HE studies HER intently. SHE hesitates, then bare-
> ly touches HER glass to HER lips.)

You're feeling all right, after what happened at our last meeting?

FIONA

I don't know how to explain....

CROWLEY

Has that ever happened to you before?

FIONA

I don't know. Sometimes I have trouble remembering things. It—
upsets me terribly.

CROWLEY

Don't let it trouble you. You have a very unusual ability, and like all
abilities, it must be cultivated. I can help you.

FIONA

Do you think so?

CROWLEY

Yes, I do. Drink your wine.

> (SHE tastes the wine. HE sips his wine and continues to study HER intently.)

I feel I know you through your writing. How is it that we have never met before?

FIONA

I don't see people. I don't go out.

CROWLEY

Your poems and stories have made you quite famous. You would be made much of in society.

FIONA

That would frighten me. I shouldn't know what to say. I shouldn't dare speak.

CROWLEY

But you are never at a loss for words in your writing. Your writing is alive with imagination.

FIONA

I hope for a time when imagination shall lay aside words and outer dress and express itself in spirit and the thoughts which are beyond words.

CROWLEY

I should like for you to speak to me that way—without fear, without the need for words and outer dress. That is the only real communication between a man and a woman.

FIONA

I wouldn't dare speak—what is in my heart.

CROWLEY

But in your poetry, your drama, your stories—you dare anything.

FIONA

Yes. But there I have only to speak to myself. It is so much easier.

CROWLEY

But very lonely.

FIONA

I am very much alone.

CROWLEY

It is not wise to be too much alone.

FIONA

I think—an artist must be alone to create his dreams and visions—must return to the desert....

CROWLEY

To the desert?

FIONA

Yes, to solitude—to that wilderness to which the creative imagination must go as the sea mew to the foam and wind....

CROWLEY

It sounds very lonely and windswept.

FIONA
(SHE has forgotten CROWLEY and is in a world
of HER own.)

Solitude is a dangerous and enchanted land, where terror walks with beauty. Where dreams start affrighted from quiet pools as the shadow of invisible fear falls past their shadowy hair. Where the vulture has her eyrie and the hyena wails.

CROWLEY

Where are you now?

FIONA

Forgive me. I have said too much....

CROWLEY

No. I want to know all about you.

FIONA

But how can you know, when I don't know myself?

CROWLEY

We could make that discovery together.

FIONA

I—am not sure you would understand...that anyone would or could understand.

CROWLEY

I want to understand if you will let me.

FIONA

I think—I belong to Amadan-Dhu, one of the Hidden People.

CROWLEY

The Hidden People?

FIONA

Yes—the Dark Ones—whose touch is madness and death for any mortal—whose falling shadow causes bewilderment and forgetfulness. They are ancient and dreadful gods—mysterious and powerful spirits—the shadows of pale hopes, forgotten dreams, and madness.

CROWLEY

Madness?

FIONA

They are a living force—elemental gods in whose lost Eden an ancient tree of knowledge grows whose fruit is Love and Spring and Death.

CROWLEY

You believe in these elemental gods?

FIONA

I believe—that they are invincible and indestructible. That they come unsought and have no need of human conventions.

CROWLEY

Yes, I know those gods. They are beyond human law, beyond good and evil...

FIONA

...neither moral nor immoral, but simply all potent and all powerful.

CROWLEY

It cannot be wrong to yield to such a god!

FIONA

To yield may be wrong, but if so, then it is wrong to yield to the call of hunger, the cry of thirst, the whisper of sleep, the summons of death.... I think I have said too much....
                    (Pause.)
Will the others be here soon?

CROWLEY

No.

FIONA

Oh. They aren't coming.

CROWLEY

Do you care?

FIONA

Did Mr. Yeats really send me the note?

CROWLEY

I sent it to you. You and I are the only ones meeting here tonight.

FIONA

I—think then—that I should go.

(SHE rises. HE also rises then takes HER hand.)

CROWLEY

No—I don't think so.

(HE kisses HER hand.)

FIONA
(Quickly withdrawing HER hand.)
Oh, don't do that!

CROWLEY

But I wanted to do that. Have you ever been kissed before?

FIONA

No—I—I must go. My cousin is expecting me.

CROWLEY

No, he isn't expecting you.

FIONA

But—he knows where I am.

CROWLEY

He doesn't know where you are. You would not tell him you were coming here.

FIONA

But, I must—let him know where I am. He will be—very upset.
He will be....

CROWLEY

Frightened? For your safety?

FIONA

Yes! Frightened!

CROWLEY

Are you afraid?

FIONA

Afraid?

CROWLEY

Yes—of me?

FIONA

Afraid...? Why should I be afraid—of you?

CROWLEY

Why indeed.
            (HE slowly draws HER to HIM and takes HER in
            HIS arms. HER back is to the audience so that the
            audience cannot see HER face. HE lifts her veil and
            starts to kiss HER. HE stops, looking down on HER
            in surprise. Suddenly startled, HE steps back.)
Who—are—you?

FIONA
            (Desperation in HER voice.)
Yes—who am I?
            (CROWLEY quietly studies HER.)
Oh, you despise me! You think me ugly!

            (SHE buries HER face in her hands. CROWLEY
            draws HER hands away from HER face and, raising
            HER chin, looks intently into HER eyes.)

CROWLEY

On the contrary! I think you are the most fascinating woman I have ever met!

FIONA

Do you—still want to kiss me?

CROWLEY

Why—yes, of course, my dear Miss Fiona MacLeod. Why not?

(HE slowly kisses HER.)

LIGHTS FADE TO BLACKOUT

END OF SCENE TWO

ACT II: SCENE THREE

(It is the following afternoon in the meeting room of The Order of the Golden Dawn. The double panels to the Inner Vault are closed. MAUD is alone.)

CROWLEY
(Entering DR.)
What a lovely afternoon. Miss Gonne, you're looking especially charming.

MAUD
I see you received the message from Willie.

CROWLEY
I assume we received the same message.

MAUD
Bram called for me, and we came at once.

CROWLEY
Where is Stoker now?

MAUD
He had to ring the theatre to tell them he'd be late. He went to the call box on the corner. Do you have any idea what this meeting is about? What is so urgent?

CROWLEY
The Golden Dawn seems to have a crisis on its hands. Here I am, but where is our crisis. Does it involve you, Miss Gonne?

MAUD
I hardly think so.

CROWLEY
Just checking. You arrive with Stoker, but your devoted poet is not part of your entourage. A little tiff between lovers?

MAUD

I hardly think that is any of your affair.

CROWLEY

But is it still *your* affair?

MAUD

You delight in making perverse remarks. You seem to assume that shock is a substitute for wit.

CROWLEY

How amusing that my poor little phrases could shock a society incapable of being shocked by its own hypocrisy.

MAUD

I am no hypocrite.

CROWLEY

No? A hundred years from how, they will laugh at our thin veneer of respectability. We have so repressed and fragmented every normal emotion that a whole man speaking the truth is labeled a "monster."

MAUD

Are you an example of the "whole man" or of the "monster?"

CROWLEY

Would you care to find out, Miss Gonne?

MAUD

I think not, Mr. Crowley.

CROWLEY

That is a pity. You and I are very much alike.

MAUD

You and I—alike?

CROWLEY

Yes. We both want power. We simply use different weapons to achieve it. You use your beauty and I—my charm.

(MAUD laughs derisively.)

Oh, yes, you may laugh. You use the power of your beauty to charm Yeats. He is your magic mirror where you see yourself beautiful, noble, and true—a complete woman. You don't dare let him get too close for fear it would shatter the illusion.

MAUD

Are you deliberately trying to be insulting?

CROWLEY

You see, we live in a society where truth is labeled "insult." And that odd view is not seen as the perversity it really is.

MAUD

And you would be a fit judge of the morals of society, I suppose.

CROWLEY

No, only of my own. I would not presume to judge you—who support dynamite as a means of social reform.

MAUD

I, at least, do not seek power for its own sake but only to support the Irish cause.

CROWLEY

Like so many others, you imagine you can go half way to power. You can no more go half way than you can jump out of a burning building and stop in mid-air.

MAUD

When it comes to the Irish cause, I shall not stop half way.

CROWLEY

Just so. You and I are the new wave of the future. You want it all—

feminine mystery and masculine power—and so do I. If our search for power threatened to blow up the earth and annihilate the sun, I don't think either of us would turn a hair.

>   (There is the SOUND of voices off. YEATS, FLOR-
>   ENCE, and STOKER enter DR. FLORENCE and
>   MAUD exchange a glace but do not greet each oth-
>   er.)

Why, my dear Mrs. Emery. You're positively radiant. Isn't she, Miss Gonne? Crises must agree with you.

                         MAUD

Willie! Are you all right?

                         YEATS
                    (Tersely.)
I'm all right.

                         MAUD

Then why all this urgency?

                         YEATS

I received a message from Sharp. He said it was a matter of life and death. He demands that we meet with him at once, or he'll call the police and have us all arrested.

                         MAUD

Is he out of his mind?

                         YEATS

So it appears. This obviously has something to do with his cousin's initiation.

                        FLORENCE

She must have told him what happened.

                         YEATS

What time is it?

STOKER
(Looking at HIS pocket watch.)
Almost four o'clock.

YEATS
He should be here at any moment. He said four o'clock.

(There is a KNOCK off. YEATS exits DR.)

CROWLEY
"The clock strikes midnight—when ghosts walk."
(To FLORENCE.)
Have you buried any ghosts, my dear, who might rise from their graves?

FLORENCE
We are not amused.

CROWLEY
Oh, but, my dear, it's all very amusing. You don't know how amusing it really is.

(YEATS reenters DR followed by SHARP, who is dressed as when earlier seen and is carrying a cane.)

YEATS
As you can see, Sharp, we are all here. Since you spoke of a matter of life and death, we'll cut short the amenities if you don't mind.

SHARP
(Trying to control HIS tension.)
I am not in the mood for amenities. I demand to know where you have taken my cousin!

STOKER
I can assure you that I, for one, have not seen Miss MacLeod since the night of our meeting.

FLORENCE

Nor have I.

SHARP

Nor have I! I demand to know what happened at that meeting!

MAUD
(Suddenly defensive.)
What—what right do you have to question us?

YEATS

Before we answer your questions, I think you should answer ours.
You owe us an explanation.

SHARP

The explanation is very simple. My cousin is missing, and your
group is obviously responsible!

YEATS

That is a serious charge. I'd be very careful if I were you. Just what
do you mean, your cousin is missing?

SHARP

Missing, I tell you! Missing! Surely the meaning is clear! Something
has happened to her! I know it! I've been nearly out of my mind.
She left this note, which I found in my study this morning.

(HE takes out a letter and hands it to YEATS.
YEATS studies it.)

STOKER

For God's sake, man, read it out loud!

YEATS
(Reading.)
"By the time you read this, I shall have gone away. I must have time to
think. Do not try to call me back again until I come forth of my own

free will. Whatever happens—you are closest to my heart. Your cousin, Fiona." Yes, the note appears authentic. I recognize her handwriting.

STOKER
According to this note, she went of her own free will.

YEATS
(To SHARP.)
On the face of it, your charge of a "matter of life and death" seems wildly exaggerated.

SHARP
Do you call suicide "wildly exaggerated?"

YEATS
This isn't a suicide note.

SHARP
You don't know her as I do. I know that she has thought of suicide.

STOKER
But the note only speaks of her "going away" to think things out.

SHARP
(Increasingly agitated.)
If she had not become involved with The Order of the Golden Dawn, she would never have gone away. She has never done anything like this before. I demand to know what happened to her! I demand to know what happened at your meeting!

MAUD
That is none of your business!

YEATS
Under the circumstances, I will speak directly about our meeting. Something unexpected did happen. It was not part of our ritual. Just after your cousin was initiated, she appeared to go into a trance.

SHARP

A trance?

YEATS

Has she been in a trance before?

SHARP

(Somewhat evasively.)
What do you mean?

YEATS

Moments when she isn't herself. When someone appears to speak through her voice.

SHARP

Nonsense! I've told you she is very shy, very withdrawn. She spends long periods by herself—away from the world.

YEATS

Yes, but more than that. A genuine trance state where another voice speaks through hers.

SHARP

Another voice speaks through hers? What are you saying?

YEATS

Your cousin appears to be a trance medium who is able to make contact with the spirit world.

SHARP

Are you out of your mind? Are you trying to malign her character, trying to absolve yourselves of blame? I place the blame where it rightly belongs! All of you are responsible! All of you are to blame!

STOKER

Steady there. No need to speak of blame. We want to help you. If your cousin is missing, we want to help find her.

FLORENCE

Of course we want to help.

SHARP

I don't believe you! It's your fault, all your fault! If she had never heard of your group, all would be as it was before.
(To YEATS, almost hysterical.)
You kept writing her, inflaming her mind with talk of hidden knowledge, of visionary experience, of other worlds. You won't get away with this! I shall go to the police! I shall swear out a warrant for your arrest!

CROWLEY
(Speaking directly and curtly to SHARP.)
That is enough! You will do nothing of the sort!

SHARP

You...! Who are you to tell me what I shall or shall not do? Aleister Crowley! The most notorious man in London! Oh, I know all about you. I have had you investigated! I have had you watched!

CROWLEY

Have you?

SHARP

Yes! And I know all about the notorious household you kept at Loch Ness! Oh, yes! Your housekeeper vanished, a workman declared insane, an infamous woman you brought from London raving in the night and selling herself in the back alleys of the village! Oh, yes, they know all about you there.

CROWLEY

Do they? Did they forget to tell you about my coachman hallucinating in the sanctuary? Scotland isn't as dull as one might think—although, God knows, it's dull enough.

SHARP

You are responsible for this! You are despicable! Degrading! You destroy everything you touch!

(SHARP suddenly raises HIS cane and tries to strike CROWLEY. CROWLEY seizes SHARP's arms, holding HIM in a powerful grip. CROWLEY is obviously the stronger of the two. THEY stand toe-to-toe, eye-to-eye, SHARP struggling to free HIMSELF. CROWLEY grabs SHARP's cane then throws him to the floor. CROWLEY pins SHARP to the floor with the cane as a sword point.)

CROWLEY

That is enough, I said. Fiona MacLeod is not missing. She is as safe as anyone in this room.

SHARP

Where is she?

CROWLEY

I know where she is—and you do, too.

YEATS

You know where she is?

CROWLEY

Yes—and so does Sharp.

STOKER

Sharp knows?

MAUD

Then why all this...?

SHARP
(To CROWLEY.)
You will regret this!

(SHARP rises to HIS feet.)

CROWLEY
I seldom regret anything. Is there anything you regret, Sharp?

SHARP
You...!

CROWLEY
It's time for you to leave now. Go while you still can. This charade
is at an end.

SHARP
I'll go, but I'll use all the influence I have to destroy you! I'll destroy
all of you!

(Like a cornered animal, SHARP glares at the OTH-
ERS then turns and exits DR.)

CROWLEY
(Lightly twirling the cane, which HE still holds.)
He'll accuse us next of having stolen his cane. His two prized posses-
sion lost in one day! How much more can a man endure?

YEATS
I have had enough of your wit!

CROWLEY
I'm rather taken with it myself. I think I should go on the stage.

YEATS
We'll discuss your pretensions another time. Where is Miss MacLeod?

CROWLEY

At the moment, I don't know.

FLORENCE

But you just said you did know.

CROWLEY

My dear, consistency is one of the weaker virtues.

STOKER

You said Sharp knows where she is.

CROWLEY

Yes, Sharp does know, but at the moment, I do not.

YEATS

Crowley, you will tell us what you know or....

CROWLEY
                    (Insolently.)
Or what?

YEATS

Or get out!

CROWLEY

And who are you to tell me to get out?

YEATS

The leader of this temple.

CROWLEY

The leader decides?

YEATS

Precisely.

CROWLEY

What if I tell you that Mathers has sent me to take over leadership of The Golden Dawn?

YEATS

Then I would judge you to be—as I've always suspected—raving mad.

CROWLEY

If you recognize Mather's handwriting, perhaps you would care to read this.

(HE takes out a letter and offers it to YEATS, who refuses to take it.)

YEATS

Do you think I would surrender this Order to you on the strength of a letter which you are perfectly capable of forging?

CROWLEY

Then perhaps our friends would care to read this letter and judge for themselves.

(CROWLEY hands the letter to FLORENCE. SHE and STOKER stand reading it together.)

MAUD
(To CROWLEY.)

If you are going to take over the leadership, I, for one, tender my resignation.
(To YEATS.)

Willie, I've been thinking of resigning for some time and have only stayed this long because of you. It is time I devote all my energies to the freedom of Ireland.

CROWLEY

Anarchy masquerading as Freedom.

MAUD

You call Irish nationalism "anarchy?"

CROWLEY

If you want freedom, you needn't go to Ireland. Remain a member of this Order under my leadership and discover what true freedom is.

YEATS

Your vision of freedom is to use people as you see fit. What happens to them is of no importance to you.

CROWLEY

You are absolutely correct. To the man of true will, there are no moral distinctions. I am free to do what I will, to think what I will, to speak what I will, and to love or hate—when, where, and with whom I will. And you are free to try to stop me—if you can.

YEATS

I will stop you from destroying this Order!

CROWLEY

And how will you do that? This Order is a microcosm for the new age dawning, and I am its prophet. Our only law—compete self-fulfillment—total freedom.

YEATS

If you are the prophet of the new age, then God help us all. You would set fire to the world in the name of freedom.

CROWLEY

Yes, and let it burn. Under your leadership, The Golden Dawn has been pretending magic. I intend to create true magic out of passion and fire. But you wouldn't know anything about passion, would you, Yeats? Sexual or otherwise. You have played at life from a safe distance—never letting it touch you, never feeling the fire burn. What do you know of passion and fire?

YEATS

If I know little of what you call passion, you know nothing of love and caring and the human heart!

CROWLEY

(Derisively.)
Love? Caring? The human heart?

YEATS

Oh, you know how to make people your wax puppets and stick pins in them, but you know nothing of human compassion.

CROWLEY

Words, words, words! I am sick of your words! Do you know what the human heart is capable of? You are human like the rest of us, Yeats. You, too, were drawn into Fiona's trance, like the rest of us. You, too, wanted to abandon control to another's will, like the rest of us. You, too, want to see what the limits really are.

STOKER

Yeats, don't listen to his raving.

CROWLEY

Raving? What are the limits to your secret desires, Stoker?

STOKER

I know my limits.

CROWLEY

What control have you abandoned?

STOKER

I never abandon control—only that one unfortunate incident.

CROWLEY

Only one incident, Stoker, out of all your secret desires?

STOKER

You don't know what you're talking about!

CROWLEY

But you know what I'm talking about, don't you, Stoker? We all know what I'm talking about. Even you, Yeats, for all your words, know the awful power of the human mind to shape the world.

YEATS

Yes, I know the human mind can raise demons and the dead and change to world.

CROWLEY
(To YEATS.)
Stoker has raised his demon. Do you have the courage?

YEATS

I will not be your wax puppet, Crowley.

CROWLEY

I challenge you, Yeats, and you, Stoker, to surrender the leadership to me, and see what the limits really are of passion and pain and human sacrifice.

YEATS

If we abandon compassion and humanity in the name of freedom, then God help the world that is being born. After us would come the savage gods.

CROWLEY

Let them come. Let them come.

YEATS

No, I won't surrender this Order to you. I won't follow you down that path. At whatever risk, we must cry out that beauty and poetry and joy must remake to world from the images of the Great Mind and Memory who is the supreme Enchanter of the world.... We

must remake the world, as if—as if we were Adam, and this is the
first morning.

CROWLEY

And your eyes shall be opened and ye shall be as gods, knowing
Good and Evil.

YEATS

You, Crowley, want to hang over the abyss and call that freedom—
and have us hang with you. Not while I'm alive.
(To ALL.)
There will be no further meetings of this Order until I give notice.
These meeting rooms are closed.
(To FLORENCE.)
Florence, as secretary of the Order, you will post the notice on the
door. Is that clear?

CROWLEY

The secretary will post whatever notice our *authorized* leader decides. Isn't that so, Mrs. Emery?

FLORENCE

Yes—just as you say. Willie, our leader, decides.

CROWLEY

And what do you say, Stoker?

STOKER

Yeats decides.

CROWLEY

And you, Miss Gonne?, do you too play "follow the leader?"

MAUD

I shall choose my own path, as I always have.

YEATS

(To MAUD.)

Yes, Maud, you always choose your own path even if it destroys you.

MAUD

(To YEATS.)

I though we were building the same Castle of Heroes. But they are different. Mine is in Ireland, and yours in another world.

YEATS

It seems to me I have spent my entire life trying to explain myself to you. But there comes a time when enough is enough.

(Turning to STOKER.)

Stoker, I'm going to get away. I have a great deal to sort out in my mind. I shall be in contact when I return.

STOKER

Very well.

YEATS

(To CROWLEY.)

Crowley, as for you—I shall give you exactly forty-eight hours. If by then Fiona MacLeod has not returned of her own free will, I shall go to the police, and that shall be my act of free will. Is that clear?

CROWLEY

Yes, perfectly. One is always free to be a damned fool.

YEATS

Yes, just what I was thinking.

(To FLORENCE.)

Florence, I have to get some papers from the office. If you will post the notice, I'll see you home.

MAUD

Willie! Where are you going?

YEATS

What business is that of yours?

MAUD

You're leaving for Ireland.

YEATS

Yes.

MAUD

Willie—please don't go without me! Please don't leave me!

YEATS

Isn't it a little late for that speech?

MAUD

No—it can't be too late!

YEATS

How many times I've wanted to hear you say that. Now, finally—it just doesn't matter.

MAUD

I don't believe that. I won't let it be too late.

YEATS

You won't let it be too late? Have you ever known how I feel?

MAUD

Oh, Willie, I know how you feel.

YEATS

Do you?
        (With sarcasm.)
Do you know how I feel, Maud? That's more than I know.
        (Now seriously, introspectively.)
That's more than I know.

(To FLORENCE.)
Shall we go, Florence?

MAUD

Please! Take me with you to Ireland...! Please, Willie...! If you have
ever truly loved me....

(YEATS turns and stares silently at Maud.)

YEATS
(Finally, contemplatively.)
If I have ever truly loved you...?
(Suddenly turning on her in verbal attack.)
If I have ever truly loved you?
(Speaking now in wrenching pain.)
You could call over the rim of the world whatever woman's lover
hits your fancy! If you come or stay—God help me—wherever I
am, you are there.
(HE reaches out and takes MAUD's hand. FLOR-
ENCE is stunned. YEATS turns to HER.)
Florence, my dear, I'm—sorry. Let me see you home.

(FLORENCE proudly draws away. SHE deliberately crosses to CROWLEY and puts HER arm though
CROWLEY's. When SHE speaks, it is in a formal
tone, cool and angry.)

FLORENCE

No, thank you. I'm sure *this*—Beast—will see me home.

YEATS

Florence—I'm—I'm sorry.

(YEATS and MAUD exit DR. FLORENCE drops
CROWLEY's arm and moves away from HIM.)

CROWLEY

Am I jilted so soon?

FLORENCE

It would seem we both are.

STOKER

I intend to go back to the theatre where melodrama is confined to the stage.

CROWLEY

And you, Mrs. Emery? What do you intend to do?

FLORENCE

To post the notice on the door. These rooms are closed, Mr. Crowley.

CROWLEY

If I might detain you for a moment longer. You both read Mather's letter. I assume you believe it to be authentic.

STOKER

Look here—I don't know what game you're playing now, Crowley....

CROWLEY

Game? Have you ever played chess, Stoker?

STOKER

I suppose you're a master of that game, too.

CROWLEY

I am—played in earnest with men and women, life and death, as my pieces.

FLORENCE

Are you suggesting that we be your pawns?

CROWLEY

You may be the queen.

FLORENCE

I will not play your game.

STOKER

I shall remain neutral.

CROWLEY

Neutral? When you joined this Order, you took one fatal step in the direction of magic. Do you imagine that you can turn back now?

STOKER

I think I have had quite enough of your magic.

CROWLEY

My magic? Every act is magical. Every act begins in the imagination before it is ever played out. Surely you know that, Stoker.

STOKER

You're the self-styled Magus, not I.

CROWLEY

Yes, and as Magus, I am calling a meeting of this Order. I dare you to see what magic can really do! Will you accept my challenge?

STOKER

I have had quite enough of you!

CROWLEY

Are you a man of courage, or are you a coward?

STOKER

How dare you?

CROWLEY

Do you dare, or *are* you a coward?

STOKER

(Stung to anger.)
I shall be at your meeting, Crowley. Name the day and hour.

CROWLEY

Tomorrow night, our ritual begins.

STOKER

I shall be there!

(HE exits DR.)

CROWLEY

And you, Mrs. Emery? Do you accept my challenge? Or is your magic confined to a stage of empty words?

FLORENCE

I have no intention of accepting your challenge!

CROWLEY

Are you really a liberated woman with a mind of your own, or does Yeats do all your thinking for you?

FLORENCE

I think that you are destroying this Order.

CROWLEY

Believe me, Mrs. Emery. Magic is a two-edged sword. I shall either lead this Order or destroy it.

FLORENCE

(Crossing DR to show HIM out.)
If you don't mind, Mr. Crowley. I must close these rooms.

CROWLEY

I can wait. I thought I might see you home.

FLORENCE

I am perfectly capable of finding my own way home, thank you.

CROWLEY

Then, if I might have just a moment of your time.

FLORENCE

It will have to be another time, I'm afraid. I'm sorry.

CROWLEY

Are you?

FLORENCE

No. I am neither sorry nor afraid.

CROWLEY

Have I, at last, found an honest woman—unafraid to speak her mind?

FLORENCE

Why should I be afraid?

CROWLEY

Why, indeed? Mrs. Emery, I admire you. You are a woman of un-explored depths.

FLORENCE

Mr. Crowley, aren't you being a bit obvious?

CROWLEY

Obvious?

FLORENCE

You want to seduced me so that I will join in with your plans.

CROWLEY

That is only one of the reasons.

FLORENCE

I already know the other. You want to use me against Willie. You think because he has not betrayed his love for Maud that I will betray him. Then you don't know me very well.

CROWLEY

Perhaps not, but I think your poet turned lover was a disappointment. Especially his making love to another woman while in you arms.

FLORENCE

How dare you!

CROWLEY

Don't try to pretend with me. You have sexual needs, sexual desires no man has ever aroused or satisfied. Certainly not your very correct husband or your misty-eyed poet.

FLORENCE

And you see yourself as having the wisdom and experience to satisfy every woman you meet.

CROWLEY

Only certain women. I'm quite selective.

FLORENCE

Am I supposed to be flattered?

CROWLEY

Yes. I want to make love to you as you were meant to be made love to.

FLORENCE

You are really too conceited. I think you'd better leave.

CROWLEY

Let's not pretend to bland hypocrisy. The world is full of bland hypocrisies, and I don't intend to waste my time mouthing one more.

FLORENCE

Yes. I see the game you are playing now!

CROWLEY

Game? Yes, it is a very old game, and I am an expert player.

FLORENCE

Yes. I see what you want. You want to keep me from telling Willie of your plans to conduct the ritual without him. Do you really imagine I will let you get away with that? I intend to send a message to Willie this very night warning him of your plans. So you see, your declaration of "lust" is a bit late.

CROWLEY

Wrong, my dear. It is your declaration of "virtue" that is a bit late. I have already made plans to see that Yeats arrives when the hour strikes. He has asked for magic, and he shall have it. Do you think I need you to trap Yeats? I shall take care of Yeats myself.

FLORENCE

Then—what do you want?

CROWLEY

To trap you, of course.

FLORENCE

Another game, I suppose. You see yourself as the dark shadow of every woman's dreams.

CROWLEY

What dream would you like to act out first?

FLORENCE

You really are too—ridiculous!

CROWLEY

If I am ridiculous, why are you trembling?

FLORENCE

I think you've said enough. Get out!
            (SHE tries to cross past HIM, but HE blocks HER
            path.)
Don't touch me!

CROWLEY

Oh, but I will touch you.

            (HE pulls HER to HIM with a hint of brutal pow-
            er, and takes HER in HIS arms in a way that shows
            HIS sexual magnetism.)

FLORENCE
            (Shaken, trying to resist.)
If you don't let go—I shall call for help!

CROWLEY

Don't bother. I shan't need any help.

            (CROWLEY kisses HER slowly and passionately.
            At first, SHE tries to resist, but then SHE responds.
            SHE kisses him passionately and then, as if remem-
            bering, again struggles in HIS arms. Having dem-
            onstrated HIS power over HER, HE releases HER,
            and SHE staggers back as if she might fall. SHE
            tries again to regain HER composure as a sardonic
            smile crosses CROWLEY's face.)

FLORENCE

What—game—are you playing?

CROWLEY
(Opens door at L.)
I intend to show you—now.

(HE holds out HIS hand, and SHE slowly puts
HER hand in HIS. THEY exit at L.)

BLACKOUT

END OF SCENE THREE

ACT II: SCENE FOUR

(A day later, just before midnight. The meeting
room of The Order of the Golden Dawn. From total darkness, the LIGHTING rises slowly. UC, the
panels are open, revealing the Inner Vault. No one is
masked in this scene, but FIONA is veiled. CROW-
LEY stands facing the altar. HE is in a long, black
robe. HE lights two tall, black candles. HE takes a
sword from the altar and holds it aloft, horizontally.
FLORENCE and STOKER enter DL. THEY also
are dressed in long, black robes. FLORENCE and
STOKER stand apart DL.)

CROWLEY
(Holding the sword aloft.)
Thee I invoke, Spirit of Osiria Triumphant, Splendour of the Glori-
fied Ra. I am He, the Bornless Spirit. All Spirits of heaven, earth,
air, fire, and water and every spell and scourge are obedient unto
me. I raise the Flame of thy Spirit with the Flashing Lightning of
My Power.
                    (HE gestures with the sword over the chalice at the
                    center of the altar, causing flames to surge up from
                    the chalice. YEATS and MAUD, in street attire,
                    enter DR. A wind enters with THEM, stirring the
                    candle and chalice flames.)
The spirits bid you enter.

YEATS
Aleister Crowley, I warned you!

CROWLEY
(Pointing the sword at YEATS.)
And I warn you! Elemental forces are abroad in this room. If you
disturb our ritual now, you endanger the lives of all here. The spirits
bid you enter. The ritual has begun.
                    (CROWLEY points the sword at the altar. The al-

tar slowly moves back, revealing a coffin-like base. FIONA, dressed in a long, gray robe and a gray veil, is lying in the tomb.

Child of Earth, long hast thou dwelt in darkness. Quit the night and seek the day.

> (CROWLEY gestures with the sword, and the figure of FIONA rises horizontally as if levitated.)

Come forth from out of the Tomb.

> (FIONA slowly sits up, hands crossed on HER bosom. SHE rises to HER feet and stands in front of the altar.)

Thou art my image, my shadow. I have made thee a creature of my thought and of my will. Child of the Earth, long hast thou dwelt in darkness. Quit the night and seek the day.

FIONA
(In HER feminine voice.)
Dweller on the earthly plane, what do you seek?

CROWLEY
I seek the sorcerer's knowledge and insight and power.

FIONA
(In HER feminine voice.)
And what, beyond words, do you seek?

CROWLEY
To be—totally free.

FIONA
(Feminine voice.)
And to this end, you have made me a creature of your thought and your will.... Made me in your image—your shadow?

CROWLEY
To this end.

(As FIONA silently examines CROWLEY, SHE seems to grow in strength and stature.)

FIONA
(In a deep, eerie voice.)
Dweller on the earthly plane, *you* stand in *my* shadow!
(FIONA's presence has become commanding, and CROWLEY's suddenly tentative.)
All that you seek, you shall find. You shall gain knowledge and insight and power.... But the hunter shall become the hunted.... Come forward and gaze in the glass.
(CROWLEY positions HIMSELF to look into an unseen glass.)
What do you see?

CROWLEY
I see a blind man on a helmless ship—without a compass—on a stormy sea.

FIONA
(Deep, eerie voice.)
Who is this blind man?

CROWLEY
Old—near death—wretched, friendless, and alone. Blind eyes staring into the darkness.
(As if gazing into those eyes.)
I know those eyes. They are my own.
(Now derisively.)
This is the comedy of Pan,
that man should think he is the hunter,
while the hounds of Love and Death hunt him.
In the savagery of the hunt then live and die!
Thus shall God's laughter be thrilled with Ecstasy!

FIONA
(Deep, eerie voice.)
Old—near death—wretched, friendless, and alone, your blind eyes
staring into the darkness. All that you seek, you shall find.

CROWLEY
So be it.

FIONA
(Turning the YEATS, in deep eerie voice.)
Dweller on the earthly plane, what do you seek?

MAUD
(In terror, seizing YEATS's arm.)
No! Don't let her speak!

YEATS
(Hushing MAUD, then stepping forward.)
Who are you...? Who are you?

FIONA
(In HER own feminine voice.)
I have come hither, led by dreams and visions,
And know not why I come, and to what end,
Mid the noise of chariot wheels
Where the swung world roars down the starry ways,
The Voice I know and dread is one with me...
As the uplifted grain and wind are one.
Though a dark wood I have come where
Dark birds, like demons, haunt the wood.
Hail, ye unknown, who know me!
(Now in deep, eerie voice.)
What do you seek? Speak now.
Whatever you seek, you shall find.

YEATS
(Entranced.)
I—seek—a key.

FIONA
(Reaching our as if giving HIM an imaginary key, speaking in a deep, eerie voice.)
Here is the key. Open the door.

YEATS
(Stepping forward, entranced, reaching out as if opening a door and walking through it. The LIGHT-ING suggests the phantom of a doorway and a path hovering in the air as if leading to another plane of existence.)

FIONA
(Deep, eerie voice.)
What do you see?

YEATS
(HIS words are based on an earlier vision which later became the subject of HIS poem, "The Second Coming," published 1921.)
I see—figures—gazing at their shadows in the tide. Storm clouds rise up over a vast and endless desert. In the distance—a dark shape moves—with the body of a Beast and the head of a man—a gaze blank and pitiless as the sun. The figure turns—a dark tide of blood rises and engulfs it all.

FIONA
(Deep, eerie voice.)
You shall take the images that haunt your dreams and make of them charms against loss and night and time, but you will never hold the woman you love nor she you until you die. This is the sacrifice you must make.
(To both YEATS and MAUD.)

Come forward and gaze into the glass.
>   (MAUD steps forward. SHE, too, has become en-
>   tranced. SHE and YEATS look into one another's
>   eyes.)
What do you see?

                              YEATS

I see—an old woman, deaf and blind, her face—old as time, lined
and full of age—all her friends and lovers dead and gone, her life
spent in empty words, empty deeds, with nothing changed.

                              FIONA
>   (Deep, eerie voice.)
Look closer. Who is she?

                              YEATS

I do not know. I have never seen this face before. A face—stark and
gaunt—the eyes of an eagle—sharp, cruel, and cold.

                              FIONA
>   (Deep, eerie voice.)
Look closer now. You have seen her face before.

                              YEATS

Whose face is this?

>   (MAUD leans forward to look closer. Realizing that
>   SHE is seeing HER own face, SHE gasps in terror
>   and covers HER face with HER hands.)

                              MAUD

Oh, my God! It is *my* face!
>   (Desperately to YEATS.)
But in the mirror of your eyes, I was always young.

YEATS

All things turn to barrenness,
In the dim glass the demons hold,
Gaze no more in the bitter glass.

MAUD

No—no!

(SHE again buries HER face in HER hands.)

FLORENCE
(Holding out HER hand as if to comfort MAUD,
but not touching HER.)

Sister, friend, do not weep. Life is but a little sleep. Everything changes. Everything passes away.

(SHE moves forward, entranced.)

FIONA
(Deep, eerie voice.)

Where are you?

FLORENCE

Walking on a cliff above the sea.
                    (The LIGHTING suggests cliffs and the sea. There
                    is the momentary SOUND of sea gulls far away.)
I am on the edge. Only one step more—and I will fall into the dark waves...far, far below. I step out—and walk on air....
                    (SHE moves forward, following HER vision.)
I hear the voices of children singing....
                    (Faint SOUND of children singing.)
I smooth the habit of my nun's gown and sit quietly, listening to their song.

(There is a peaceful smile on FLORENCE's face as
the song fades.)

STOKER

(After foreshadowing indications during the forego-
ing, HIS darker side abruptly taking command.)

You fools! Your world is full of maggots feasting on rotten flesh! You
are all worms and food for worms, feeding on the maggot heap of
the world!

FIONA

(Deep, eerie voice.)

Spirit out of the shadows of time—speak.

STOKER

Why do you call me from my hiding place? You, with your pale
faces all in a row like sheep in a butcher shop! You shall be sorry you
called me out, each one of you!

YEATS

Stoker!

STOKER

Stoker? That pompous fool? I have more bodies than just this one.
My revenge is only begun. I spread it over centuries—and Time is
on my side!

CROWLEY

Who are you?

STOKER

You know who I am...! You have summoned me, Crowley—and I
am here!

(With malevolent sarcasm.)

You would be the Beast?

(STOKER motions for CROWLEY to come closer.
HE is projecting HIS spell, focusing it on CROW-
LEY.)

Gaze into the mirror of my eyes and see the monster you shall become!

(Caught up in the spell, CROWLEY looks into STOKER's eyes. So irresistible is the energy STOKER is concentrating upon CROWLEY that CROWLEY at first falters—then abruptly breaks away in an abject display of cowardice. Escaping from STOKER's stare, CROWLEY crosses toward FIONA, and STOKER turns to follow.)

YEATS
(Approaching to intervene.)
Stoker!

STOKER
Stand back, you fool! Or it shall be worse for you! Stand back, all of you!

FIONA
(Deep, eerie voice.)
Stop! I command you!

STOKER
You command *me...*? How dare you call me from the darkness into the light?

(STOKER springs at FIONA, HIS hands at HER throat. YEATS attacks STOKER, attempting to pull HIM away from FIONA. YEATS's strength is no match for the possessed STOKER's. FIONA slumps to the floor. MAUD and FLORENCE scream in terror. CROWLEY stands upstage, visibly struggling to reassume HIS customary stance of superiority to it all. As FIONA's body strikes the floor, there is the SOUND of thunder, and the doors blow open and shut. The possessing spirit leaves FIONA, and simultaneously withdraws from STOKER, who falls into a desolate, kneeling posture center stage. ALL find themselves released from the spell. FLOR-

ENCE hurries to turn up the LIGHTS. YEATS hurries to FIONA's side, but CROWLEY intervenes.)

                    YEATS

Is she hurt?

                    CROWLEY

I don't know.
                (YEATS approaches CROWLEY and FIONA.)
Stand back!

                    YEATS

But we must get help.

                    CROWLEY

No, wait! Don't call anyone!

                    YEATS

If she's hurt, we've got to help.

                    CROWLEY

She may be dead.

                    MAUD

Oh!

                    FLORENCE

Oh, no!

                    STOKER

Oh, my God! What have I done?

                (FIONA begins to stir.)

                    YEATS

She's all right....

CROWLEY

Stand back, I tell you! Leave her alone! Don't touch her!

YEATS

Are you mad? She needs our help!

CROWLEY

If you want to help, leave her alone!
> (FIONA slowly sits up. Then, holding onto the altar, SHE struggles to HER feet, dazed. SHE manages to stand, leaning against the altar.)

Fiona MacLeod, I command you not to speak!

FIONA/SHARP

> (In feminine voice.)

You command me not to speak?
> (The voice now that of WILLIAM SHARP.)

Who are you to command me?
> (HE removes the veil and wig, revealing the head of WILLIAM SHARP.)

You have destroyed her, and you command me not to speak? Oh, but I will speak. She was all good, all gentleness. She lived only for her visions, and you've destroyed her. You couldn't leave her alone. She came to me in the night through a doorway of moonlight in the spirit of a woman. She was all beauty and gentleness and love—the only beautiful thing I've ever known. She lay with me as a woman with a man. She I were one, body and soul, the same spirit, the same joy, the same love. For days after, my breasts swelled and were one with her breasts.
> (Pause.)

And now you've destroyed her! You couldn't let her live! You couldn't let her alone to be what she had to be! You had to control her, to use and degrade her! You had to destroy her! You who think you know all the answers. You had to destroy her! She was my life, my soul, my only joy. The only beautiful spirit I have ever known. And now, she sill never be free again.

CROWLEY

If I call her forth, do you think she will not come?

SHARP

Yes. She would. I know her well. But if she ever leaves my house again—if you ever touch her again—I will kill her with my own hands. I promise you that.
(To YEATS.)
Fiona MacLeod is no longer a member of The Order of the Golden Dawn. I hereby place her resignation in your hands.

(SHARP, not removing HIS robe, exits DR.)

YEATS
(To CROWLEY.)
You bastard! You knew William Sharp and Fiona MacLeod were one and the same, and yet you let this happen!

FLORENCE

You would sacrifice any of us if it served your purpose.

CROWLEY

Yes, but I didn't know which of us would be the sacrifice. It appears we all are.

FLORENCE

You have killed Fiona MacLeod! Murderer!

CROWLEY

We are all murderers. If you go down your path, Florence, you must sacrifice the sensual and journey to a far land where I can never follow. Would you give up what you seek to bring Fiona back to life again?
(FLORENCE does not answer.)
I thought not.

YEATS

You are the one who has murdered Fiona!

CROWLEY

Have I, Yeats? You will never hold the woman you love, nor she you, until you die. But you *will* be a great poet, and she will move the minds and hearts of men. But the spiral paths you tread, you each will go alone. Would you give up what you seek to bring Fiona back to life again?

(YEATS and MAUD do not answer.)

I thought not.

(To STOKER.)

Stoker, whatever dark desires you seek, you will find them. Would you give up what you seek to bring Fiona back to life again?

(ALL are silent.)

No? I thought not.

(In desperation, STOKER pulls off HIS robe, hurls it to the floor, and hurriedly exits DR.)

Our leader was looking for a key, I believe. I shall leave you my key to these rooms.

(CROWLEY drops the key to the floor at YEATS's feet.)

YEATS

You needn't bother. I intend to have all the locks changed.

CROWLEY

After tonight, I don't think anyone will want to get in.

YEATS

Do you imagine these dusty rooms contain our dreams? The golden dawn is in the human heart and the divine imagination, and there, it's just the hour before dawn.

CROWLEY

Then the hour is late.

(Turning to FLORENCE.)

Shall we go, my dear?

(HE holds out HIS hand to FLORENCE. SHE

draws back, refusing HIM.)
Are you to become a saint? I should be sorry to lose you from the ranks of us sinners.

(To ALL.)
Dear friends, you'll forgive me if I take my leave. Never fear. We shall meet again.

(CROWLEY had moved downstage while speaking. The OTHERS have remained upstage. Facing THEM, CROWLEY makes an elaborate bow, then, in a sweeping motion, HE turns to face the audience. The upstage LIGHTING dims, and a bright FOLLOW SPOT highlights CROWLEY.)

Never fear, we shall meet again—in a new dawn!

(CROWLEY repeats HIS elaborate bow, this time to the audience.)

BLACKOUT

END OF THE PLAY

Appendix

The Golden Dawn
Productions and Readings / Awards and Honors

Productions
1992, Hamline University, St. Paul, Minnisota
1988, Detroit Center for the Performing Arts, Michigan

Readings
1988, Southern Theatre Conference, Atlanta, Georgia
1988, Detroit Center for the Performing Arts, Michigan

Awards and Honors
1992, Chosen, Hamline University Competition, St. Paul, Minnesota
1991, Finalist, Florida Studio Theatre Contest
1991, Finalist, West Coast Ensemble Contest, Los Angeles, California
1989, First Place Winner, Southeastern Theatre Conference New Play Competition
1988, First Place Winner, Pepperdine University National Playwriting Competition, California
1988, Finalist, National Playwrights' Conference, O'Neill Center, Connecticut
1988, Finalist, Lee Korf Playwriting Awards, Cerritos College, California

About the Authors

Jan Henson Dow has won more than 150 national playwriting competitions, awards, and honors, including an NBC New Voices Award. Her plays have received numerous productions, workshops, and staged readings around the country, and her full-length plays have been published by Samuel French and Popular Play Service.

As a Professor at Western Connecticut State University, Dow directed the Playwriting Workshops and co-produced Western's Festival of New Plays. She has been the recipient of a number of playwriting grants, as well as grants for the new play festivals. She also taught playwriting workshops at the Osher Life Long Learning Institute at the University of South Carolina and at workshops around the country. Her articles and poems have appeared in such publications as *The New York Times*, *The Dramatists Guild Quarterly*, *Kansas Quarterly*, and *Indiana Review*. She co-authored *Writing the Award Winning Play* with Shannon Michal Dow, and they have just completed their first novel, *The Darkest Lies*. Jan is a member of the Dramatists Guild.

Robert Schroeder has won a number of playwriting competitions, including an NBC New Voices Award. His plays have been staged nationally. He served on the staff of *The Dramatist Guild Quarterly* and the Dodd-Mead *Best Plays* reference annuals. His reviews and theatre commentaries also appeared in *The Nation*, *Commonweal*, *New York*, and other periodicals. His anthology, *The New Underground Theatre*, was published by Bantam Books, and he was among the contributors to *Playwrights, Lyricists, and Composers on Theatre*, a Dodd-Mead hardcover. He has been retained professionally as a play/musical "doctor" for a number of Off Broadway productions.

Phosphene Publishing Company publishes books and DVDs relating to literature, history, the paranormal, film, spirituality, and the martial arts.

For other great titles, visit
phosphenepublishing.com

www.ingramcontent.com/pod-product-compliance
Lightning Source LLC
Chambersburg PA
CBHW071348170626
46811CB00003B/1041